Thomas Swift

The Life of Saint Winefride

Virgin and Martyr

Thomas Swift

The Life of Saint Winefride
Virgin and Martyr

ISBN/EAN: 9783744664349

Printed in Europe, USA, Canada, Australia, Japan

Cover: Foto ©Raphael Reischuk / pixelio.de

More available books at **www.hansebooks.com**

THE LIFE OF ST. WINEFRIDE.

THE LIFE OF
SAINT WINEFRIDE

VIRGIN AND MARTYR.

Based on the Acts Compiled by the Bollandist Fathers.

EDITED BY

THOMAS SWIFT, S.J.

———

BURNS AND OATES, LIMITED.

London :
28, Orchard Street, W.

New York :
Catholic Publication
Society Co.

———

1888.

PREFACE.

———

"ST. WINEFRIDE, most admirable virgin, even in this unbelieving generation still miraculous, pray for England."

Thus do we pray in the Litany of Intercession for the conversion of our country, and it seems certain that Divine Providence designs the marvellous cures so constantly occurring at St. Winefride's Well to bring back many to the Church of their forefathers. Meanwhile, the devotion of catholics towards this great Saint appears to be waning. Pilgrims to the Well are not so numerous as of old, and there is less eagerness to assist at the festivals kept in her honour. Possibly, one cause of this falling off may be the little publicity given to the graces conferred and cures wrought by St. Winefride's intercession. The publication of a new Life of the Saint therefore, it is hoped, may be a means of stimulating the fervour of catholics and of leading non-catholics, to study the source of that sanctity which God glorifies in His saints.

The occasion of the present Life is the publication of the *Acta Sanctæ Wenefrede, Virginis*, by the Bollandist

Fathers, S.J. These Acts have been compiled with
the greatest care, and after minute research into all
available sources of information. Some of the results
of these investigations are given in the following
pages without wearying the reader by references to
authorities. These are all given in the original Acts.
The Life by Robert of Shrewsbury, given here in full,
was published in English in 1635, by a Father of the
Society of Jesus, but it is now hardly to be met with,
and the style is very antiquated. One quotation
from this Author's Preface may not be deemed out of
place here :

*"And if the matter of the booke, conteyning in it sundry
strange and miraculous passages, shall seeme ridiculous to
Protestants chancing to read them, it is not much to be wondered at, sithence they will be their owne choosers, even in the
very beliefe of Sacred Verities themselves, Divinely revealed ;
and sleight, as fabulous Legends, the Lives of Saints, written
by St. Athanasius, St. Ambrose, St. Hierome, St.Climachus,
St. Gregory, and other holy Fathers. It sufficed my Author,
and so it shall me, that devout Catholiques, for whose
instruction and comfort he penned first his Historie, will
piously and probably assent to that which heere is credibly
proposed unto them, avoyding two extremes eherein ; the one
is of believing things over-lightly, and the other of believing
nothing at all but as fancies and selfe-opinions do guide
them."*

It may seem strange to some that, among the many
miraculous interventions here recorded, there is hardly
any reference to spiritual graces. This is not because

such favours have not been conferred, but because the recipients of such graces are naturally more reticent about them, and because the witnesses of such favours are chiefly spiritual advisers, to whom they are entrusted in confidence. In reality, wonderful conversions are continually occurring, and no pastor can exercise his ministry in Holywell for any length of time without feeling the efficacy of St. Winefride's prayer for the souls of her clients.

May this Life be the means of leading many to seek her powerful aid in all their afflictions, whether of soul or of body, temporal or spiritual.

Holywell, November, 1887.

CONTENTS.

———

To face p. 1.

CHAPEL OVER THE WELL.

LIFE OF ST. WINEFRIDE,

VIRGIN AND MARTYR.

———

CHAPTER I.

Introduction.

THE town of Holywell in Flintshire derives its name
from the celebrated Well of St. Winefride, Virgin
and Martyr, who entered into rest about the year 660.
The place where the Well rises, and the town now
stands, was previously known as Sechnant, or the
Dry Valley, but there was no village or settlement
there of any importance before the date just given.
The town of Holywell, in Welsh Trefynnon, is situated on an eminence near the northern coast of
Flintshire and the river Dee. It contains about
nine thousand inhabitants. At the foot of the hill
rises the famous Well, the waters of which, after a
course of about a mile, during which they are used
to move the ponderous wheels of more than one
large water-mill, find their way into the river Dee.
The supply of water at the spring is extremely
copious, amounting to six hundred tuns every hour.
The water is very clear, and very cold, never rising
beyond 50° Fahrenheit in any weather. Chemical
analysis has never detected any mineral or medicinal

B

properties peculiar to it.* The stream has never been
known to have been frozen. The stones round the
source are covered with mosses of a purple hue,
which have been identified as the *Junger mannia
Asplenioides*, the *muscus subrubeus*, called by Linnæus
Byssus Iolithus, and the *Conferva gelatinosa*, all natives
of North Wales and some other northern countries
of Europe, and which gave currency to the popular
legend, formerly received, that the stones were dyed
red in the blood of the Saint. The Well is approached
by an extremely handsome portico or gateway, and a
long flight of stone steps, and is covered by a vaulted
roof of considerable height and extent, and extraordinary architectural beauty, over which rises what
was once the chapel or oratory of St. Winefride, now
used as a schoolroom for the Anglican communion.
The Well, which is public property, and held by the
Local Board of Holywell, is rented by the Jesuit

---

* Analysis of a sample of water received from St. Winefride's Well,
Holywell

One imperial gallon (70,000 grains) afforded—

Calcium carbonate	13·750 grains.
Magnesium carbonate	0·840 ,,
Calcium sulphate	4·160 ,,
Magnesium chloride	0·591 ,,
Alumina, silver, and a little iron	0·875 ,,
Potassium and sodium sulphate	0·543 ,,
Nitrogen in nitrates	0·101 ,,
Nitrogen as ready formed ammonia	0·005 ,,
Nitrogen in organic combination	0·007 ,,
Watery hydrating salt and volatile matter	3·124 ,,
Total contents	23·996 ,,

The sample as received was in excellent condition, and free from
nitrate. Its hardness was not excessive, and the water as received was
to be regarded as a wholesome sample of a moderately mineralized
supply.

J. EMERSON REYNOLDS, M.D.

March 21, 1882.

Fathers of the Holywell mission. All the buildings over the Well were erected at the close of the fifteenth century, partly at the expense of Margaret, Countess of Richmond and Derby, the mother of King Henry VII.; but the armorial bearings inserted into the sculpture indicate that several noble families of North Wales, including those of Stanley, Pennant, and Lewis, bore a share in the work. The building is of great richness and beauty, and represents, on a smaller scale, the style customary at that period, of which there is a well-known example in the chapel of Henry VII. in Westminster Abbey.

Popular belief in the miraculous properties of St. Winefride's Well has survived the change of religion, and the other changes of the times, and the Well is still frequented by pilgrims in search of health. Nor is their search disappointed, as the following pages will show. And there is still extant, or was extant at the beginning of the century, a traditional recollection of the promise given to the holy virgin by St. Beuno, that her intercession should always be efficacious, at least on a third visit to the spot sacred to her. But in other respects the tradition of the story of her life, which for some centuries after her death was clear, strong, and consistent, has died out or become confused and vague, in the lapse of ages. The only trustworthy authorities for the Life of St. Winefride, which we are about to relate, are two documents, both dating from the twelfth century. One of these, a manuscript preserved in the British Museum,* which has been translated by W. J. Rees,† gives us a brief Life of the Saint, prefixed to an account of some miracles wrought at the Well under the observation, or within the know-

---

* Cotton. Claud. A, 5.   † *Lives of the Cambro-British Saints.*

ledge of the writer, who seems to have been a monk of the neighbouring monastery of Basingwerk, the ruins of which still exist some two miles to the north of the town. The Life appears to be an older record, preserved by this writer, and has been erroneously, and without any ground, attributed to St. Elerius, her director. Its authorship is quite uncertain.

The other Life of St. Winefride, which is much fuller and more complete, is from the pen of Robert, Prior of Shrewsbury, who was subsequently chosen Abbot of his convent in 1140, in the reign of King Stephen, and was written apparently in 1137. The most complete copy of this manuscript, and probably the original, is preserved in the Bodleian Library at Oxford. There are other copies, less perfect, in the Royal Library at Brussels, and in that of Trinity College at Cambridge. There is a third history, included in the *Sanctilogium* of John of Teignmouth, and published in Capgrave's *Nova Legenda Angliæ;* but it is evidently an abbreviation of the work of Robert of Shrewsbury, and gives us, therefore, no fresh information. All these documents, and all other information of every sort bearing on this subject, are collected with immense accuracy and industry, by the Rev. Father Charles de Smedt, S.J., the Bollandist compiler, and form a portion of the *Acta Sanctorum* for 3rd of November, the day on which the festival of St. Winefride is observed. It is greatly to be regretted that our space does not admit of our placing the whole account in the English reader's hands; but the following epitome will give, it is hoped, all that is most important.

We will proceed to lay before the reader, as nearly as possible in their own words, first the narrative of the monk of Basingwerk, and then that of Robert of Shrewsbury, reserving any remarks they suggest until the reader has perused them, and merely remarking here (1) that Robert of Shrewsbury does not seem to have seen the older record; and (2) that the two accounts, independent of one another, agree in all important particulars except one, specially noticed by Robert, viz., the Saint's pilgrimage to Rome, which he rejects. He will himself inform us as to the sources from which his information is derived.

CHAPTER II.

Life by a Monk of Basingwerk.

HERE BEGINS THE LIFE OF ST. WINEFRIDE, VIRGIN
AND MARTYR.—If it is good to hide the secret of a
king,* no less is it irksome to refrain from publishing
the great deeds of God. I have accordingly undertaken, by the help and favour of God, to write down
what the tradition of older times has handed down
to us regarding the *Blessed Winefride*, to the praise of
God, and the exhibition of her exalted merit—for
they are things well worthy to be left on record.

There lived, in the days when Cadwan was King
of North Wales, a famous chief named Teuyth, son
of Eylud, who was the possessor of three manors
in Tekeynglia (Flintshire). His three manors were
respectively named Abeluyc, Mayngwen, and Gwen-
fynnon. Teuyth had no son, and one only daughter,
whose name was Winefride ; and who, from her
earliest years, fixed her whole affection upon the
heavenly Bridegroom, and dedicated her virginity to
Him alone, rejecting in anticipation all mortal aspir-
ants to her affections or her hand. Her father, being
made aware of this resolution, could not but feel some
regret that his daughter's renunciation of marriage,
as she was his only child, made it impossible to
preserve his inheritance in his own line. On the
other hand, he could not but rejoice to think that his

* Tobias xii. 7.

child had given herself to God, and the chief accordingly determined to secure her such an education as
should fit her for the life on which she proposed to
enter.

While he was under the influence of his resolution,
the blessed prelate Beuno, having been driven forth
from his own dwelling by the pressure of the numerous
branches of the house of Selym, took refuge at the
house of Teuyth and continued to reside there. The
chief, finding him to be a learned and religious man,
consulted him about his daughter and asked his
opinion as to how she should be educated. Beuno
listened to his account with great attention, and said
to him : " If you will make over your estate to God,
in trust to me, I will live here with you, and instruct
your daughter in the law of God." To this Teuyth
replied : " My lord, there is no one who would more
willingly do this, if it were in my power. And, if the
time were not too long, I would ask you to remain
here while I go to the king and obtain his consent to
the arrangement you propose." He answered : "Go,
my dear son, and God go before you to give you good
success." Teuyth accordingly proceeded to the residence of the king, his lord, and earnestly entreated
his assent to the disposition of his patrimony which
he proposed to make. The king's reply was in these
words : " Reverend man, it stands neither within my
right nor yours to alienate your patrimony from the
public service of the State and of the community.
But I give you permission to dedicate any one you
like of your three manors to the service of God, pro-
vided you will leave me the other two."

Teuyth hastened home with this favourable reply,
which he reported to Beuno, and added : " If, therefore, you wish to remain with me, you are now at

liberty to choose out of any part of my inheritance
the spot which pleases you best." The blessed Beuno
then said : " I should prefer to dwell in the solitude of Beluye." And so it was done. Beuno, with
Teuyth his patron, built a cabin in the valley called,
in the language of the Britons, Sechnant ; erected
there a little church, in which he said Mass daily,
and daily gave instruction to the maiden Winefride
in the Sacred Scriptures. Teuyth and his household
assisted every day at the office of the Mass, and
Beuno always followed it with a catechetical address.

One Sunday, it happened that Teuyth and his wife
had gone early to Mass, while Winefride still remained
at home, in order to bring with her the fire, water,
salt, and other things required for the Holy Sacrifice.
Just then Caradoc, son of Alaucus, a prince of royal
birth, who had been out hunting wild beasts, came
weary with the chase, and very thirsty, to ask for
drink. Reaching the house, he inquired who was its
owner ; but he had, also, another purpose which was
beginning to form itself in his mind. The girl, being
alone in the house, went at once to greet him, and
answer his inquiries respecting her father, and grace-
fully saluting him informed him that her parents were
gone to hear the preaching of Beuno at Mass. Caradoc gazed at the fair and rosy complexion of the
maiden, and admired her beauty of face and figure,
which was very great. His heart began to burn with
desire for her, and leading her into the house, where
they were alone, he forgot his thirst in the vehemence
of his love. " Dearest maid," he said, " listen to my
entreaty, and allow me to become a recognized suitor
for your hand. I love you most earnestly." To this
the maiden replied : " My lord, such words of com-
mendation should not be addressed by a man of your

rank and lineage to a humble maiden such as I am. Indeed, I cannot do what you request. I am betrothed to another, whom I am just about to wed." This reply filled Caradoc with fury. "Away with such trifling and folly," he exclaimed, "and consent to my wishes. I will make you my wife." The girl was now seriously alarmed at his violence, and set her wits to work to devise a means of escape. "Allow me," she said, "to retire for a few moments to my chamber and change my dress, that I may be fitter to enjoy your society. I will leave undone the task entrusted to me, and place myself at your disposal." Caradoc answered: "If you will promise not to be long, I will wait a little while."

Thankful for the reprieve, the girl passed quickly through the chamber and ran down into the valley, anxious only to conceal herself and get out of his sight. Caradoc soon discovered that she had deceived him, and furiously angry, mounted, set spurs to his horse, and went off in pursuit. The girl had all but reached the door of the monastery, where she hoped to obtain protection from God and from Beuno, and was just about to step across the threshold, when he reached her with his sword and cut off her head.

Her parents saw it, and were for some time in a stupor of astonishment and grief. When they recovered from this, their tears and sorrow were pitiable to witness. Beuno also witnessed the tragedy, and, overwhelmed with grief, left the altar and came to see who had done this murderous deed. Raising his eyes he saw Caradoc, standing with his bloody sword in his hand; and, perceiving him to be the murderer, he cursed him as he stood. The miserable man melted away before their eyes, like wax before the fire. Beuno went to the corpse of the dead girl, carrying

her head, which had rolled inside the door, and
earnestly beseeching God to restore her to life, lest
his enemy should triumph over him, he fitted the
head to the body. His prayer was heard. The body
returned at once to life and animation, only showing
a slender scar running all round the neck. And on
the spot where her blood had flowed there was an
earthquake, with a loud noise, and a great stream of
water burst forth, and has continued to flow from
that day to this. The stones in that stream have
been ever since, and are still, the colour of blood ; the
moss has the scent of incense, and is a remedy for
various diseases.

Beuno, understanding that God had wrought this
miracle on her account, said to her, in the hearing of
her parents : " My sister, God intends this spot to
belong to you. I must go elsewhere, to the place
where God has appointed that I am to end my days.
I have a request to make to you, which is, that you
will send me every year a cloak made by your own
hands." " My lord," she said, " I will very gladly
do so, but I am afraid I shall have very great difficulty
in sending it, especially as I do not know where you
are going to live." To whom the holy man answered :
" Have no anxiety on that point. There is a stone
in the middle of the river, on which I have been
accustomed to meditate and pray. Put the cloak
upon this stone when the day comes round, and if it
comes to me, let it come." Thus, with mutual bene-
dictions, they parted.

The blessed Winefride lived for many years in
that solitude, as Beuno had advised her. Once
every year, on the vigil of St. John Baptist, she
sent a cloak to Beuno, in the manner he had indi-
cated, laying it out upon the stone, and the stone

carried it down the stream, dry outside and in, out
into the sea, and by sea to the harbour of Sachlen,
and to the hands of Beuno. Thus Beuno every
year received the maiden's gift. And the merits
of the virgin imparted to the cloak this virtue,
that wherever Beuno wore it the rain never wetted
him, nor the wind moved his hair. Hence he went
by the name of Beuno of the Dry Cloak.

About this period, as is related, Winefride went
to Rome to visit the sacred resting-places of the
Apostles, and devoutly offer herself wholly to God
in presence of their relics. This done, she returned
to her desert. In those days the holy men of all
Britain assembled in the Synod of Winefride, and
Winefride, with other saints, also repaired thither.
By this Synod all the institutions of religion were
fixed and settled, that is to say the saints who had
previously lived singly and dispersed, with no rule
but that which their own will imposed, were collected
in suitable dwellings, with a view to the improve-
ment of their mode of life, under experienced
superiors placed at the head of each house. Thus
it happened that blessed Winefride was appointed
to preside over eleven virgins, who received from
her the pattern of holy conversation. The bearing
and eloquence which she displayed surpass our
powers of description; her language, and the
thoughts she expressed are said to have been
sweeter than honey and purer than milk, to the
apprehension of those who listened to her. Hence
she was always called White Winefride; for she
spoke with the whiteness of wisdom, and lived in
faithful and constant observance of her vows. The
spot where she dwelt with her maidens is called
Gurtherin. And there, when her course was ended,

she fell asleep, and was buried on the eighth day
before the Calends of July, and with the virgins her
companions rests in Christ, to Whom is honour and
glory for ever and ever. Amen.

Here ends the Life of St. Winefride, Virgin and Martyr.

CHAPTER III.

Some Miracles recorded in the above Life.

HERE follows an account of several miracles which
occurred at the Holy Well, and to which we will
refer presently: but one or two brief historical
notices will enable the reader better to understand
the foregoing history, as well as the longer one
which is to follow.

The name Winefride is in Welsh, Gwenfrewi.
The syllable *Gwen* means *white*, and an explanation
has been given above, and another is given below,
of the application of this term to our Saint. Winefride is an English name. Winfred was the original
name of St. Boniface, the Apostle of Germany; and
in the document just quoted we have mention of
the Synod of Winefride, which Father de Smedt
supposes to be a meeting of the Bishops held at
York in 660 for the consecration of two British
bishops, under the presidency of the Saxon Bishop
Wini, when some statutes were passed for the regu-
lation of monastic discipline. Some have thought
that St. Winefride, from her bearing this name, must
have been an Englishwoman. But this was not
the case. She lived long before the time when the
English made any conquests in Wales; and the

English name of Winefride has been substituted for her Cambro-British name Gwenfrewi to suit English ears, very much as the Irish names Tiernan and Maol Ceachlin have been softened into Terence and Malachy.

Cadwan, King of North Wales, was the father of Cadwallon and grandfather of the great Cadwallader. These three princes extended their dominion over the whole of Wales. Cadwan is said to have reigned from 607 to 634. According to the best information that can be obtained, St. Winefride was born about 610, and died about 660. It is somewhat uncertain who Caradoc was, and one high authority suggests that he may have been a son of an Armorican prince, in alliance with Cadwan, then visiting Wales. There was at that time frequent communication between the two countries. Histories similar to the liquefaction of the body of Caradoc occur in the Lives of St. Cadoc, St. Iltutus, St. Paternus, St. Lasrian, and St. Colman of Dromore. Of the resuscitation of women who had been beheaded, in the same manner as St. Winefride, Father de Smedt says that he has met with no fewer than twelve examples in the lives of Cambro-British saints. The flow of fresh springs of water at the prayer of the saints is of frequent occurrence in the hagiology of many countries, and in Wales particularly it is attributed to St. David, St. Iltutus, and others, and there is another instance of it in the Life of St. Beuno. The story of the cloak conveyed across the water on a rock, is met with also in the Life of the Irish St. Lenanus, who received in this manner a cloak sent to him by St. Dermicius. In the Life of St. Winefride which follows there is no mention of the stone, and the cloak, wrapped in a cloth, is conveyed upon the surface of the waves. St. Beuno's Stone, a flat rock some three feet across, is still to be seen in a pool adjacent to the Fountain, and there is no reason to doubt that it is the spot where he was accustomed to pray.

The sons of Selym, whose multiplication occasioned St. Beuno's leaving his home, were the grandsons of Conan, King of Powys, one of the three ancient divisions of Wales. There is no other record of the convent founded by St. Winefride at Holywell, except this; but the spot where it stood is pointed out by local tradition, two and a half miles from the town, towards the north-west; nor is there any other mention of the convent at Gwytherin, where she ended her days. The only extant Life of St. Beuno is one in Welsh, translated by J. W. Rees in the *Cambro-British Saints*. The monastery where he ended his life was situated at Clynnog, nearly opposite the coast of Anglesea, and his tomb was preserved until the beginning of the present century. The village of Bodfari, Henllan, and Gwy-therin, mentioned in the following narrative, are all in the county of Denbigh, and within a circuit of ten or twelve miles of the town of that name. St. Chebius, in Welsh, Cybi, is commemorated on the 6th of November. His Life is given by Rees, *Cambro-British Saints*. St. Lenanus is believed to be the same with the famous Irish Saint of that name, the 1st of March. There are churches dedicated to him at Llansannan in Denbighshire and Bedwellty in Monmouthshire. There must once have been a church at Gwytherin under the invocation of St. Elerius, but it does not now exist.

The monastery at Shrewsbury, to which the relics of St. Winefride were transferred, as related in the

following account, was founded in 1083, for which
see Ordericus Vitalis. It would seem that the see
of St. Asaph was at that time temporarily suppressed, or united with Bangor. The Prince of
Wales reigning at the time of the translation was
either Gruffydd, son of Conan, or his son Owen, who
succeeded in 1137.

———

CHAPTER IV.

The Life of St. Winefride, and the Translation of
her Relics. By Robert, Prior of Shrewsbury.

PROLOGUE.

HERE BEGINS THE PROLOGUE TO THE LIFE OF
ST. WINEFRIDE, VIRGIN AND MARTYR.—To my Lord
and Father Warren, the Reverend Prior of Worcester, his son Robert, in life a sinner, Prior of the
Convent at Shrewsbury, wishes grace to walk without stumbling in the way of the commandments of
the Lord. Those whom the Divine mercy has permitted to become the depositaries of any portion of
truth, are bound by the debt of religion and charity
to impart what they know to others, as long as those
others are desirous of becoming acquainted with the
counsels of God. That which comes from Heaven is
the common inheritance of all men of good will, if
they deserve it, and tends to further their salvation.
Therefore, Rev. Father, I will not keep from you
the knowledge of the good things which have been
poured forth upon us from on high, and which I
know you will receive with joy and exultation. I
send you, therefore, my lately-written Life of the

blessed virgin Winefride, collected partly from detached writings,* preserved in the churches of the district where she lived, and partly from the narration of priests, whose veracity is recommended by their venerable age and by the habit they wear. And I was induced to write partly by the fear of God, lest the talent entrusted to me should be found to have been buried in the earth, and never put to use ; and partly by affection for this holy maiden, and desire that she should obtain from the faithful the honour due to her merit. I have purposely suppressed what related to her pilgrimage to Rome, and some other particulars current in popular report, because I did not find them recorded in writing, and the persons who told me these things were not always men upon whose authority I could place sufficient reliance. I have endeavoured to write the clearest and simplest narrative I could, and this I know you will approve. I have, indeed, not to lengthen my history too much, omitted some particulars which I thought true, because I consider that I have given enough to set the life and character of this most holy maid clearly before the reader, and I hope that by her intercession and your prayers I shall obtain from God's mercy the reward of the toil I have expended on it.

* Schedulas.

CHAPTER V.

St. Winefride, under the guidance of St. Beuno, set on fire by the love of Christ, consecrates her virginity to God.

THE LIFE OF ST. WINEFRIDE, VIRGIN AND MARTYR.

In the western portion of the island of Great Britain, is the province called Wales, bounded on one side by the frontier of the kingdom of England, on the other by the sea. This region was in old times the abode of a multitude of saints, of great and diverse merit, and is adorned to this day with innumerable privileges and memorials which recall their names. Among these saints was a holy man of great fame and eminence, whose name was Beuno, highly distinguished for sanctity even among so great a multitude of saints. Leaving his native place, trampling on the pride of the world, shunning its perilous temptations, he fled in absolute poverty, became a monk, and soon began to lead a perfect life in Christ. Having founded churches, and gathered together congregations of brethren devoted to the service of God, in more than one place, he was directed by an admonition from Heaven to go elsewhere, and seek another spot in which to dwell. Led by the Spirit of God, Who directed his steps to the future benefit and advantage of numbers yet unborn, he arrived at the seat of a powerful chieftain named Theuith, who was the son of a senator of the highest rank next to

c

the king, named Eliuth, and who considered that he
was doing honour to the traditions of his noble birth
by maintaining his household and establishment in
suitable elegance and splendour.

The venerable Beuno, coming to the house of this
chief, was by him kindly and respectfully enter-
tained. He lost no time in explaining to his host
the motives of his journey, and calling him aside,
said to him: " My lord, I am sent to you by an
instinct which comes from on high. I have lived in
many places, and have never failed to find a place of
residence which suited my purpose and inclination ;
yet my spirit nowhere found rest ; the Spirit of God
continually urged me to seek a fresh abode. Leaving, therefore, the habitations in which I took most
pleasure, I come now to you, ignorant for what purpose the Divine will, which foresees that which is to
come, has directed me hither. I am sure that these
things are not accidental, nor is there any doubt that
all things are ordered by the command of God, that
man's purpose is made the instrument of the execution of His decrees. If you will accede to my wishes,
you will further your own salvation by patiently
considering the proposal I am going to make. I ask
you to concede to me some portion of your patri-
monial estates, that I may build a church in which I
may serve God, and pray daily for your salvation."

The chieftain, who had perceived him to be a man
worthy of praise and veneration, was already prepared to yield to his wishes ; and his reply was to
this effect : " It is only right and just to pay back to
God a part of the gifts He has bestowed upon us, in
gratitude for His beneficence. I owe you also gratitude for making this request to me, and am not
ignorant that it is in my own interest to grant it.

Come, therefore, and take what you demand. I give
you up this villa in undisturbed possession, free from
all liabilities to myself or my successors, and devoted
to the service of God only. I have a daughter, my
only child, on whom all my joy and all my hopes
have heretofore exclusively rested. I wish to commit
her education to your charge, and desire you to pray
the Lord to dispose her way of life to His glory and
my true honour, and that I may live to rejoice in
her." Without delay he made over the estate to the
holy man to build a church, and the accommodation
required for the servants of God who were to reside
there, removing himself and all his effects to another
spot, whence he had the dwelling of the holy man in
sight, and could behold it at any hour of the day.
The Saint thus speedily obtained his wish.

The chief not unfrequently laboured with his own
hands in the construction of the church, and constantly attended to it, supplying the expenses and
encouraging the workmen. He was also often present
at the celebration of the Divine Mysteries, with his
wife, and with his daughter, whose name was Winefride. And when the man of God announced to the
people the Divine commands, he placed the young
maiden at his feet, desiring her to listen attentively
to all she heard, and receive his words in her heart.
And God, Who foresaw what was to come, did not
permit all this to be in vain. The maiden, destined
to be herself God's temple in after years, listened
eagerly and affectionately to what she heard, and
stored it all in her memory. She often asked and
obtained permission from her parents to seek the
man of God at other times, and thirstily drank in the
words, sweeter than honey, which fell from his lips.
And though her parents both loved her tenderly, and

the only hope of the transmission of their line rested in her, yet they rejoiced to see her attend to the Saint's discourse, for the better preservation of her chastity with a view to marriage, which they contemplated for her. But the mercy of God inspired her with a nobler ambition than she yet realized. Daily she advanced in sanctity and wisdom, and God's Spirit filled her heart and mind. Gradually she resolved to put aside all thoughts of man, and long only for the embrace of God; but hesitated to make this resolution known to her parents. She thought she ought not to oppose them; and yet she knew that it was best for her to be united wholly to God. She was aware that both her parents wished her to be married for the sake of continuing the line of their house; yet she knew with still greater certainty that it was far better to offer herself a chaste virgin of Christ.

This conflict in the mind of the young girl occasioned her no little uneasiness. On one side the fear of displeasing her parents kept her from her purpose, on the other the love of God powerfully impelled her to put it in execution without delay. Her master had recited to her the words of the Lord, commanding her to leave her father and mother and follow Christ; but she was as yet too young to take the vows. At last she resolved upon doing this, if no other way was made clear to her for the accomplishment of her holy purpose; but she thought it best to obtain the intervention of the man of God with her parents, in the hope that with the aid of God's grace she might thus bring them round to her view. She went to him, and told him her secret wish. "You have sown the seed of the Word of God," she said to him; "I wish you to see what has grown up from it. I have determined to abandon the luxury and splendour of the world, and preserve my maiden-hood whole and undefiled for the honour of my Heavenly Bridegroom. And for this you, most holy Father, must obtain for me the consent of both my parents."

The Saint was deeply moved by such an evidence of piety, and rejoicing that Divine grace had brought forth such fruit as this, promised to speak earnestly to her parents on the subject, and do what in him lay for the accomplishment of her wish. He found his task easier than he had expected. The parents of the girl reposed such full confidence in him that they were entirely under his guidance; and the sweetness of heavenly things, which they ardently desired all mankind, and especially their daughter, to experience and enjoy, had taken full possession of their own minds. When they were made acquainted with his wishes, they blessed God with abundance of tears, and readily granted his request. They pro-ceeded to lay aside a burden which had long weighed heavily upon them, their earthly possessions, which they distributed to the poor; and they expended upon the Divine Offices the sum they had set apart as a dowry for their daughter, in the event of her marriage. Freed from the cares of the world, they gave themselves up wholly to the commands of God, walking in the path of justice, and never turning aside.

The maiden herself was overwhelmed with joy at attaining the great desire of her heart. Rejoicing in the Holy Ghost, she sat for some time as a postulant at the feet of the man of God, listening eagerly to all he told her of the glory of her Heavenly Spouse. Left to do as she pleased, she ran with dilated heart

in the way of the commandments of God, forgetting
the things that were behind, and stretching forth to
those which were before. For love of Him to Whom
she had devoted herself, she allowed in herself
nothing that was of earth, desiring only, like the
prophet, to dwell in the house of the Lord all the
days of her life. She did not wait for her parents to
conduct her to the church, but went early in the
morning to be present at the Divine Mysteries; not
unfrequently she watched there all through the
night. Sometimes she would break in unseasonably
upon the holy man, and desire to hear more about
her Bridegroom, what He was like, and what He
did. Loving Him with her whole heart, she was
delighted to hear any one speak of the excellency,
power, and splendour of her Heavenly Lover. She
took more delight in this than in any pleasure the
world could afford her, and it left an unfailing senti-
ment of joy and delight within her heart. Young as
she was, she was already grey in mind and character,
and had no desire left for anything but God; girl as
she was, she was a man in the perfection of every
virtue. Exteriorly, as well as in her soul, she was
endowed largely with the gifts of God; she was fair
to see, affable to speak to, modest and composed in
all her movements. Nor did these graces fail to
expose her, as we shall see, to the wiles and strata-
gems of the cunning enemy of souls. Earnestly
engaged as she was in the work of her salvation, the
devil could not but perceive that his power and
dominion were likely to be severely shaken through
her means, and desisted not from his machinations
until he thought he had prevailed, and that she could
do him no further harm, which happened in this
way.

CHAPTER VI.

Her Martyrdom and Resuscitation to Life.

SOLICITED TO SIN BY A PROFLIGATE YOUNG MAN NAMED
  CARADOC, SHE ESCAPES FROM HIM AND HER HEAD IS
  CUT OFF. SHE IS RECALLED TO LIFE BY THE PRAYER
  OF ST. BEUNO, AND A FOUNTAIN OF WATER MIRACU-
  LOUSLY SPRINGS UP ON THE SPOT WHERE HER HEAD
  HAD FALLEN.

THE blessed Beuno completed the building of his
church, with God's help, and when it had been dedicated to God, the people in the neighbourhood began
to resort to him ; and the parents of Winefride came
every day to hear him speak of the things of God.
One Sunday, while every one was on the way to
church, and the parents of the maiden were gone to
hear the preaching of the holy man and to attend
Mass, their daughter, being sick, was compelled to
remain at home. A young man named Caradoc, son
of King Alan, entered the house, and found her seated
near the fire. She recognized the king's son, and
rising, gently asked him what he wanted. He inquired
where her father was, and said he wished much to
speak to him. She said : " My father is gone to the
church, to assist at the Divine Mysteries, and if it is
necessary for you to see him, you must wait a little
while till he returns." She said this in perfect simplicity, and without a suspicion of any evil design on
his part ; but, in fact, his evil passions had brought

him thither, and now hurried him on violently to the
accomplishment of his wishes.   He replied : " I will
wait patiently for his return if, meanwhile, you will
be kind to me, and consent to what I wish.   You
know I am a king's son, and can endow you with
wealth and honours, if you will agree to my request."
She then perceived his intention and, with a blush,
cast down her eyes ; but with great presence of mind
she pretended to be distressed because he had found
her in her simple and ordinary dress.   After a pause
she said to him: " You are a king's son and, by God's
permission, will one day be a king yourself: and I
have no doubt you would surround me with every
earthly happiness if I became your wife.   Yet, wait
till my father comes, and I, meanwhile, will go to my
chamber and quickly return to you."   Her only object
in saying this was to get away from him for an hour.
For she could see that the unhappy young man was
nearly wild with his unholy passion, and almost tor-
tured to death by it.   Her parents' absence made
him dangerous, and she exerted all her ingenuity to
find a means of escape.   He permitted her to go to
her room, in the expectation that she would speedily
return to him more handsomely dressed.   She rose,
entered the chamber and, without an instant's delay,
went out by another door, and ran as fast as she could
towards the church, where she hoped the presence of
the congregation, if not the fear of God, would afford
her protection.

The ill-starred youth soon found out that she was
gone and, furious at her escape, seized his sword and
made after her.   The house was at some little distance
from the church, and he overtook her without much
difficulty. Staring savagely at her, he thus addressed
her : " Once I loved you, and desired to hold you in

my embrace. You have fled from me when I came
to you; you reject the suit I made to you. Yield
now to me, or else this sword shall put an end to
your life, for I will cut off your head." The maiden
looked towards the church, to see if any one would
come out, but no one appeared. Then she turned to
him and said: " I am betrothed to the Son of the
Eternal King, the Judge of all mankind. No other
spouse can I receive; no other will I have while I
live. I should outrage Him otherwise. Draw your
sword, and exert all your strength and ferocity; but
be sure that neither terror nor flattery, promises or
threats, will ever draw me away from the sweetness
of His love, to Whom my own love and devotion are
pledged." The licentious prince heard that he was
despised, and well knew that she would keep her
word. His passion overmastered him; he felt he
could never know a moment's rest while she was
alive. He drew his sword from the scabbard, and
cut off her head. And the moment the head fell to
the ground, and on the spot it touched, a copious
spring of the purest water gushed forth, and continues
to flow to this day, giving healing to multitudes
through the merit of this blessed maiden. The head
rolled into the church, which was close by, the body
falling outside, for the church was at the foot of an
incline, on which the two had been standing, down
which the head rolled, while the body remained
where it had fallen.

The head rolled among the feet of the people
standing in the church and attending at the Divine
Mysteries. There was a cry of dismay and horror;
all exclaimed at the enormity of the crime, and called
out for vengeance on the perpetrator. The girl's
parents heard the commotion and, running to the

spot, asked what had happened. They saw their daughter lying dead, and her head cut off, lying at their feet, and they both fell to the ground, amid tears and lamentations, overwhelmed with horror and grief. There was great confusion in the church, all lamenting the virgin's death, and many deeply compassionating the misery of her unhappy parents. Into the midst of the tumult the holy man came from the altar, and seeing the maiden whom he was about to consecrate to God so cruelly murdered, expressed the profoundest sorrow and compassion. The murderer still stood outside, wiping his sword upon the grass, in sight of them all. Being the king's son, he thought he could not be punished for the crime, in the commission of which he had forgotten all fear of God. This pride and hardness of heart, glorying in the deed he had done, was more than the Saint could endure, and going up to him, with the maiden's head in his hands and looking into his face, he said to him:

" Wretch, who have disgraced the generosity of youth and the honour of regal descent by so foul a murder, do you not even repent the deed? Having broken the peace, outraged the Church, horribly offended God, are you not sorry for what you have done? Then, since you spare not the Church, and have no reverence for the sacred day of the Lord's Resurrection, I pray my God that you may this instant receive the reward due to the crime you have committed." The young man fell to the ground, and instantly expired; and, to the astonishment and terror of all the beholders, his body melted away and disappeared. Many asserted that they saw the earth open and swallow him up, so that his body seemed to go down with his soul into the pit of Hell.

The Saint held the dissevered head of the young

maiden in his hands and kissed it, with tears and
anguish of soul. Recovering, he fitted the head to
the body, which he covered with his cloak, and
breathed into the nostrils. Then he desired her
parents, who had all this time seemed inconsolable,
to pause in their grief, and went himself to the altar
and celebrated Mass. This done, he returned to the
body, all earnestly regarding him and raising their
hopes to God for what they hardly dared to ask. He
addressed a few words to them, telling them that this
blessed virgin had given her vow to God, and time
only had been wanting for its fulfilment; and that
their duty now was to throw themselves on their
knees in His presence and pray for her resurrection,
in view of the benefits she would confer upon multitudes in generations to come. This they readily did,
for they were profoundly affected by the maiden's
sudden and early death and the frightful grief of her
parents. They prayed long and earnestly, and then
the holy man, rising from the ground and lifting his
hands to Heaven, said : " Lord Jesus Christ, for love
of Whom this maiden despised the things of earth
and aspired only after those which are above, merci-
fully listen to our prayer of devotion, and pour forth
the bounds of Thy piety upon us, and by Thy power
give effect, now and here, to what we desire. And,
though we know full well that this maiden, who
suffered death for Thee and is now resting in celestial
joy, is in no want of our society, nor would wish to
rejoin us here on earth, yet do Thou, most kind
Father, listen to the prayer of Thy children suppli-
cating Thee, and give assent to their petition. Let
her soul, restored to her body, prove Thee Lord of
body and soul alike, that returning to life she may
magnify Thy name, and the years of her mortal pil-

grimage fully accomplished, return with the multiplied usury of a holy life and conversation to Thee, her Spouse, the only-begotten Son of God the Father, with Whom, and the Holy Spirit, Thou livest and art glorified, God for ever and ever, through endless ages.

All answered *Amen.* The dead girl rose up as if from sleep, wiped the sweat and dust from her brow, and looked at them as they stood transfixed with astonishment and admiration. A slender scar like a white thread was visible all round her neck, marking the place where the head had been severed, and remained visible throughout the rest of her life, in testimony of the wonderful miracle of which she had been the subject. The people of those parts insist that she was called Winefride from this circumstance, for the syllable *wen* signifies white in their language, and two letters of her original name (Brewi) being changed for euphony, we thus get the name Winefride. It is also related that the white thread on the neck was plainly visible to all those to whom she was permitted to appear after her death, which is an argument to show that she was not displeased to have this name conferred upon her.

The place where her blood was spilt was originally called the Dry Valley; but from the time the fountain sprang up on the spot where her head in falling touched the ground, and which has continued to flow to this day, healing all diseases both in men and cattle, the place has been called by her name. In their language it is (Ffynon Gwenflewi), the word *ffynon* having the same meaning as the Latin word *fons*, a fountain. From the blood that streamed from her body, and flowed down the hill, the stones, both in the source of the stream and on its banks, were coloured crimson; and wonderful to relate, they still retain their crimson colour, as will be seen by all that look at them. They appear as if covered with clotted blood, which, however, no industry or perseverance can wash away. The moss which adheres to them has the smell of incense. It is well known to all the dwellers in the neighbourhood, by ancient tradition, that the fountain has continued to flow just as it did at first, and the blood-stained stones remain as a witness of the virgin-martyr's merits, and of her willingness to aid and succour all who invoke her. And the men of that region who had not as yet learned to know the true God and His justice, having witnessed the miraculous resuscitation of the holy maiden, and the evident miracle of the fountain bursting forth on the spot, threw themselves at the feet of the holy man, and petitioned to learn from him the mysteries of God. He received them with kindness and piety, purified them in the laver of Baptism, instructed them in the precepts of God, and confirmed them in His service.

CHAPTER VII.

Winefride founds a Convent near Holywell.

Departure of St. Beuno. St. Winefride founds
a convent of virgins at his church, and continues to reside there, guiding her companions
in holiness and virtue. She sends a cloak to
St. Beuno every year, conveyed to him on the
surface of the water.

We have now to describe briefly the life which the
blessed Winefride continued to lead after her resuscitation, and her end, after the completion of her
mortal term. On being raised from death she continued, as before, to sit at the feet of the holy man,
listening to his discourse, and seeking fuller instruction in the things of God. At length, having obtained
full knowledge of the rule of ecclesiastical discipline,
she urged to be allowed at once to assume the veil.
"My parents," she said, "offer no opposition, and
you know my mind, which is bent upon despising
the pleasures of the world, and longs only for the
knowledge and love of God. There is no reason
for delay, or for withholding from me the blessing
I desire. I shall not quit you, and cannot be torn
from your feet, until by your blessing I am initiated
into the mysteries of regular discipline, and my
outward habit shows me to have taken my lot with
God. Do not delay my wishes, holy Father, but
yield to my persuasion and give me what I so

earnestly desire." Then the holy man sent for her
parents, laid before them their daughter's wishes,
and intimated that he was ready to comply with
her request. Their consent was readily and gladly
given, and he received her vows and clothed her
with the sacred veil in presence of a multitude of
witnesses. She continued to advance to greater and
greater perfection, and delighted her teacher and
director by the ardour of her love to God and man.

Presently he called her parents to him, and
addressed them as follows : " It is you who received
me when I came, a stranger, listened to my request,
gave me a place of habitation for God's service, have
done all in your power to aid me in carrying it on.
God's grace has richly rewarded you. A light from
Heaven has shone upon you and your child.
Cultivate and follow it, and walk carefully in the
way it will guide you. And since God is calling me
elsewhere, and you will no longer have my presence
among you, attend to what your daughter says, for
most assuredly not to you only, but to all people in
times to come, she will be an example of salvation."
Then turning to the holy maiden : " You," he said,
" are by God's command to succeed to my labours
in this place, living in this spot, and following yourself, and exhibiting to others, the path of life which
I have pointed out to you. He has chosen you to
bear the palm of conspicuous merit in His presence,
that by the double example of your martyrdom and
your holy life, many may be brought to love and
serve Him. You must reside here and gather round
you a band of maidens devoted like yourself to God.
Yet you may hold it as certain that you will not here
end your days. For having served God here for
seven years in abstinence of body and affliction of

spirit, you will under Divine direction seek another
abode.   God will both direct your course, and
through you will illuminate the darkness of the
hearts of many.   And bear this in mind, that your
memory will be great and celebrated in the world,
and that multitudes will testify, by the healing of
their sicknesses and infirmities by your intercession,
how great were your merits before God."

The blessed maiden wept in great affliction when
she heard of the departure of her teacher, but Beuno,
taking her by the hand, led her to the fountain which
had sprung up where her head had fallen to the
earth, and making her stand upon the stone which
is still to be seen by the fountain's side, and is called
by the inhabitants St. Beuno's stone, he addressed
her in these words: " Behold the traces of your
passion.   These stones, sprinkled with your blood,
prove that you suffered martyrdom for God, for they
are still freshly reddened with your blood, to your
honour, and for a memorial of you to many that
shall come.   Now, therefore, attend to the words
I am about to say, words which will be repeated
with awe and reverence in the hearing of multitudes
of men, and will be of service and benefit to many
in the ages that are to be hereafter.   Three gifts are
given to you by God, which shall be the title of your
praise, and imprint in the minds of posterity the love
and reverence of your devotion.   These stones, red
with your blood, shall never cease to be spotted with
that blood, but in memory of your passion will retain
the hue of gore for ever, by the power of God, and
in memory of the triumph of your chastity.   Whoever
shall at any time, in whatsoever sorrow or suffering,
implore your aid for deliverance from sickness or
misfortune, shall at the first, or the second, or

certainly the third petition, obtain his wish, and rejoice in the attainment of what he asked for. And if at the third petition he fail to obtain it, he will know that he is shortly to terminate this mortal life, and for this reason, by the secret judgment of God, is denied his request, but for his soul's sake should persevere in his invocation of your assistance to obtain what is far better than anything he may have asked. And the third gift is this : when I leave you, I shall seek the habitation which God will provide for me on the margin of the sea ; and though I shall be at a great distance from you, yet the Highest has commanded that every year a gift from you shall reach my hands. Whenever, therefore, you have ready the present you intend to send me, bring it to this fountain, whatever it may be, and committing it to God, place it confidently in the water. You shall see your deposit carried down by the stream into the great river that flows below, and the sea shall obey its Maker's will, and carry your gift to the door of my retreat, across the rolling waves and amid the stormy winds, till it safely reaches my abode. And this is to be done, so God commands, every year, as long as my life continues. And these three gifts conferred upon you by God will be the seal and proof of the Divine favour that rests upon you, and will be wondered at and related by multitudes to the glory of your praise and name." He conducted he-to the church, and there said to her : " I leave to you this temple and the buildings round it, con-structed partly by my own labour, and partly at the expense of your parents, that when I am gone away, you, and the virgins whom you gather round you, may serve God as you propose, always keeping before you the example I have set you. Know that

D

in this spot there will take place a grand exhibition
of the mercy of God, to the temporal and eternal
welfare of many, and that by the example of those
who dwell here multitudes will be led to the knowledge of God, despising all the emoluments of the
world to make gain of Christ. Many will here be
healed of ailments of body and soul, and every age
and sex will here find the remedy they require.
Brute animals will not lose their share of these
benefits, for God's clemency will so rest upon this
place that great miracles will be wrought here for
the honour of your name. Therefore prove yourself
an acceptable advocate with God, and so act towards
all men that in you His holy Name may be glorified,
and you may be a means of salvation to those who
behold you. I go to serve God elsewhere, in my
humble measure, and ever while I live shall retain in
my heart, in sweet memory, the recollection of your
devotion."

He went away, taking nothing but his staff, leaving
all the furniture and whatever else God had given
him by the hands of the faithful, to the blessed maid
and her companions. One clerk alone accompanied
him; all the others he commended to God with his
farewell. But as he went he frequently stopped to
look back at the blessed Winefride, tears flowing
from his eyes at the thought that he would not
behold her bodily presence again. His words and
his departure greatly afflicted her, and her sorrow
was evident in her face, as she complained that she
was left alone and unaided, exposed to the assaults
of wicked men, deprived of the presence and affectionate care of her shepherd. And while they
endeavoured to console her, she and some others
accompanied her beloved Father in God as he left

the church, and as long as she kept up with him she was inconsolable, which the holy man perceiving, and being scarcely less moved himself, at length he quickened his steps and tore himself away, giving her his benediction with his right hand as he did so. She followed him with her gaze anxiously till he was out of sight, and then she turned home with her companions.

But after a time, recalling the mode of her conversion to God, her title to martyrdom, and the surprising predictions of Beuno, she took courage and abandoned her sorrow. She was the bride of Christ, and her whole desire was to live worthily of His heavenly affection and chaste embrace. A large number of young maidens soon came to put themselves under her charge, and not a few were induced by her example to take the religious vows, and assume the veil. She led them in strict observance of their rule, both by precept and example, always doing herself what she exhorted them to do, and persevering in fasting, prayers, and vigils. Numerous miracles accredited and seconded the exhortations she addressed to them, and God's grace conferred upon her a sweetness and eloquence of language which made her persuasions irresistible. They all rejoiced and glorified in a superior who was so visibly endowed with celestial grace, and upon whom there seemed to rest a light which came direct from Heaven. All the people of the neighbourhood were brought by her example to the love of devotion; those at a greater distance rejoiced in her fame and honour, and in the miracles which God wrought by her hands. The wild and untutored populations of the Welsh mountains were softened and subdued by her gentleness, and numbers fixed their residence in her immediate neighbourhood, so that the spot she dwelt in was no longer a solitude, but grew into a town.

Blessed Winefride never lost sight of the recollection of her beloved master and teacher, and as the anniversary of his departure drew near, she took care to prepare the present he had desired her to send him. She made a cloak, with the willing aid of the maidens who were under her charge, and early on the morning of the day on which it was to be sent, which was the 1st of May, she repaired with many others to the fountain side, carefully wrapped the garment in a white cloth, and placed it in the water, saying that she intrusted it to the stream for conveyance to the blessed Beuno. And wonderful to relate, incredible except to faith, the parcel was not wetted by the water, and the stream carried it, dry and uninjured, down into the broad estuary of the river Dee. All that day and the following night it was borne forward by the waves, and in the morning was cast on the shore close by the spot where Beuno had fixed his habitation. In the morning, when Beuno came out of the church, he stood for some time on the shore, admiring the expanse of waters, and watching the ebb of the tide, when his eye was caught by the folded cloth left on the shore by the retreating waves. He went forward and raised it, unfolded the cloth wrapped round it, and found the cloak unharmed by the waves; even the outer cloth was perfectly dry. Reflecting on the cause of this phenomenon, the memory of the maiden Winefride beloved of God, came into his mind, and he recognized that in obedience to his command she had sent him this present, which the waves had carried to him unharmed. He gave thanks to God,

and laid up the gift in his church, for his own use
and that of the other servants of God. And he
rejoiced especially and greatly because she had been
mindful of his words, and because her fame was
spread throughout all that country. And he prayed
that the Lord would bestow upon her the increase
of all virtue, that whatever was pleasing in His eyes
might be found abundantly in her, and that the
consciences of others might through her be enkindled
with devotion towards Heaven.

And it appeared by the event that these prayers
were heard and answered. For the love of heavenly
things carried her so far that she appeared in herself
a sum of all perfection, and was like a bright ray
from Heaven illumining all the country with the
perfect example of a holy light, both those who saw
her and those who saw her not. She had a way of
persuading every one, which seemed miraculous and
divine. All the people of the country abandoned
whatever she warned them to abstain from, and
applied themselves eagerly to the works of faith
which they learned from her, and saw practised by
her and the virgins under her charge, while she
carefully and minutely carried out all the instructions
she had received from the blessed Beuno, omitting
nothing. Every year, on the 1st of May, she sent
her present to her master, in the manner described,
as long as he lived; and he always found it next
morning cast up by the waves at the door of his
monastery. From this circumstance the holy man
obtained the name by which he is known throughout
Wales, to this very day, Beuno Casul Sech, that is,
Beuno of the Dry Cloak, because it was carried to
him dry through the waves. After a few years he
left this world, and migrated to celestial joy, at an

advanced age. The story of his life and death, the actions of his earlier years, and the miracles wrought at his intercession after his death, are kept on record, and retained in the reverent and affectionate memory of the people, and are remarkable in this, that the miracles which followed his death are much more numerous than those he wrought during his life.

CHAPTER VIII.

Journey to Gwytherin.

After the death of St. Beuno, St. Winefride is directed by Divine revelation to St. Deifer, and by him to St. Saturnus, and by him to St. Elerius at Gwytherin, and there enters the convent presided over by St. Theonia.

Having heard of the death of her master and teacher, St. Winefride mourned and prayed for him, and no longer sent her annual present. She began to be sensible of the loneliness of her situation and felt as if she was deprived of all human aid. Several of her companions had died; she began to be weary of the place in which she lived. Then there came into her mind the words of her beloved teacher, who had told her that after seven years she would remove elsewhere. She left off building, and all similar undertakings, and her spirit found no rest as long as she continued to dwell in that place; though she felt that she could not actually leave until the seven years were fully run out. But, when the seven years were expired, she felt herself free, and understood that she must determine her own course on her own responsibility.

She therefore addressed herself to God in earnest prayer, entreating Him to direct her where to go for her own advantage and spiritual profit, and that of others; and that He would send His blessing on the spot where she had lived, so that all who resorted thither, either for prayer or remedy for sickness or trouble, might obtain what they sought on invoking her name, and by the intercession of those who had devoted themselves to a spiritual and holy life in that place. How this prayer was heard is proved unmistakeably by the testimony of innumerable multitudes who have been relieved of their infirmities at that spot, as will be shown by many examples which we will proceed to cite, when we have brought this story to a close.

While the blessed Winefride was earnestly engaged in prayer, entreating God's mercy to guide her in her way, one night, while she was watching and praying, a message from Heaven sounded in her ears, to this effect : " Take one of your maidens to accompany you, and go to the blessed Deifer, who lives at the place called Botavarrus (Bodfari), and consult him as to what you are to do, and where you are to go." He was a great man before the Lord, walking in all His commandments and justifications blameless. It is related of him that, filled with the grace of supernatural power and virtue, he made a fountain of water spring up out of the ground, and, extending his hand over it in blessing, prayed God that any sick man who bathed in that stream might return home cured and in health, and the efficacy of his prayer was proved by great numbers of people who in this way obtained restoration to health. Many miracles are recorded of him as wrought during his life, but one which occurred after his death is especially worthy

of being mentioned, as exhibiting the abundant efficacy
and value of his merit. A band of thieves going forth
to plunder, found two horses in the cemetery where
the blessed Deifer was interred, and took them away
with them, thinking to escape without difficulty. The
owners subsequently came to the cemetery and, not
finding the horses, concluded that they had been
stolen. They returned home and made some candles,
with which they entered the chapel of the confessor,
and placed them upon the altar. The candles were
not lighted, and they had no means of lighting them,
and they therefore prayed the Saint of God either to
light them by a ray from Heaven, or else accept their
devotion as it was intended. But the Saint, as if to
show that he accepted their offering and petition,
suddenly lighted the candles in their presence. This
increased both their devotion to St. Deifer and their
hope of recovering their lost property by his means,
and in this hope they were not disappointed. For
the thieves wandered all over the neighbourhood, and
about midnight, having lost their way, looked about
them to discover where they were. They found themselves at the fence of Deifer's cemetery. They were
much disturbed at this discovery, for they knew well
that if they were caught they would have a severe
penalty to pay for their crime. Accordingly, they
rode off again as fast and as far as they could. But
the hand of God was still upon them. Day broke
and they found themselves once more in front of the
gate of the cemetery, where they had dismounted,
and were holding their horses by their bridles; at the
very moment when the owners of the lost steeds
came forth from the oratory, where they had spent
the night, in confidence of Divine assistance coming
to them in the morning, and caught them with the

stolen property on their hands. They recovered their horses, and let the thieves go; but the circumstance illustrates the merits of the holy man to whose advice the blessed Winefride was divinely instructed to have recourse.

The most holy maid, accordingly, committing to God's care the habitation and the companions whom she was leaving, and taking one of them with her, as directed by the oracle, sought the abode of blessed Deifer, which was about eight miles distant, and was by him kindly received. Having prayed long, they sat down, and the maiden explained the cause of her coming. The holy man answered her: "I am at present profoundly ignorant of God's design in this; but have patience, and remain here this night. Perhaps God will reveal His will to us, and fulfil your wishes." To this she readily agreed, for the oracle from Heaven had plainly signified to her that this holy man was to direct her what to do. All that night he continued in prayer, as was his wont; and as he prayed, he heard a voice from Heaven saying: "Tell My beloved child, the virgin Winefride, to go to the village of Henthlant (Henllan), where she will in part obtain what she wishes. She will there find a venerable man, named Saturnus, from whom she will learn more fully what to do, and where to fix her habitation." In the morning the holy Deifer called the maiden, and told her all that had been said to him, pointed out to her the route she was to follow, and bade her follow it joyfully, for it would lead her to the accomplishment of all she wished.

The blessed Winefride accordingly, rejoicing that all doubt was now removed, and that she was certainly under the protection of God, set out to visit the blessed Saturnus, who received her with every mark of kindness. He had already been warned of her approaching visit, and of its object, by a voice from Heaven, and requested her to remain there that night, promising to give her full direction in the morning. When the morning came Saturnus said to her: " There is a spot called Witheriacus (Gwytherin), honoured by the relics and the memory of many saints, and beloved by God and reverenced by men for the holy lives they are leading or have led. There it is God's will that you shall dwell for the remainder of your days, and by your example animate and inform the minds of others. The abbot, whose name is Elerius, is a man of great virtue, whom continual groaning and per-severance in prayer have so purified and set free from earthly cares that he feels no longer the ambitions or pleasures of the world, but is intent only on Heaven. To him I am commanded by God to direct you, and to assure you that you will there find all that is sufficient to satisfy in this life a soul which only longs for Heaven. There are there virgins dedicated to God, who even from their infancy have been brought up in the observances of the religious life, and attend to them with careful devotion. To these your admonitions and example, with God's blessing, will bring profit and improve-ment. Watchful as they are in the service of Christ, your coming among them will render them still more devout, and a brighter splendour from on high will rest upon them."

Hearing of the holy life these virgins led, she at once professed her desire to join them, and asked for a guide that she might set out without delay. St. Saturnus sent his deacon with her to show her the way, and himself accompanied her for the beginning of her journey. He told her much of the pleasantness of the new home she was seeking, and when at length he left her, at her desire, he gave her his blessing. The holy Elerius, who was notified of her approach by the Spirit of God, came quickly part of the way to meet her, and received her as a most faithful worshipper of God, while the deacon repeated all that his superior had desired him to say, and told in what way God had made manifest His will that she should seek that spot. Greeting her with great reverence and affection, the Saint first conducted her into his church, and his prayer completed, embraced and exhorted her to courage. Then taking her aside, he asked her what were her own intentions and idea. " For," he said, " although the course of your life, the way in which you were initiated into the Divine mysteries, and how you obtained the title of martyrdom by decapitation, and the shedding of your blood, all this has been made known to my humility by Divine manifestation. I wish to learn from your own lips the cause which has induced you to take the trouble to travel so far." She replied : " He Who revealed to you the things you have condescended to tell me, has not, I think, left you totally in ignorance of what I wish and of my object in coming here. The power which revealed to you the past concerning me, can also reveal to you the future. Receive me, therefore, as one committed to your charge by Heaven, and dispose of my mode of life according to the tenour of the Divine command which foreshadows it to you." The holy man deferred his communication until the morrow, begging her to wait patiently till the time came.

St. Elerius remained all that night in prayer, and the blessed Winefride prayed with him. About day-

break the certitude of this matter was made manifest
to him as he slept, and rising he came to her greatly
rejoicing, and again embracing her, bade her dwell
in joy and security thenceforward. Then he took
her by the hand and led her into the convent, where
he addressed the inmates in these words : " Attend,
my beloved daughters; for what I have to say is
worthy your attention. The Divine clemency has
condescended to adorn and illustrate you with a
great splendour. He has destined this maiden,
devoted to Him, to remain and live among you,
that by witnessing her life you may become more
devout in His service, and her reward be given her in
Heaven for the improvement she will be the means
of effecting in you. This is the virgin Winefride,
whose fame has often reached your ears, who to
preserve her chastity inviolate despised at once the
violence of the enemy and the enticements of the
flatterer, and gladly suffered death to keep her
virginity unharmed. Yes, this is she, the standards
of whose triumph gleam throughout the Church, and
in whose title of martyr all our country glories, as
an honour and blessing. She alone will obtain, and
is not ignorant that she will obtain, from the hand of
God, the palm of a martyr and an illustrious confessor, both in one. She comes to dwell among you
until the day of her death, whose merits have already
reached Heaven, and for whom a place of reward
among the blessed martyrs is reserved on high.
Receive her joyfully, and embrace her devoutly as
a celestial treasure, and in all things seek to aid and
imitate her. For to this end the Highest has sent
her hither, that by copying her you may lay up your
merits beside hers in Heaven, and that this spot may
become celebrated on her account as long as the

world shall last." Turning then towards one of
them, who was his own mother and the superior
of all the religious, he said to her: "To you, dear
mother, I especially commit the care of this maiden,
beloved of God. Follow her footsteps, imitate her
deeds, follow her counsels. For know, and let it
be known, to all who are seated here, that this
blessed maiden has been sent hither by special
command of God, on which account you are bound
to show special devotion to her, and understand from
this proof of it, the care which God has for your
house." The holy confessor departed, and the blessed
Winefride remained thenceforward with the handmaidens of God.

From that time she seemed bent on storming the
very citadel of religion, and bringing every virtue to
the highest perfection, as if heretofore she had been
nothing but an alien to sanctity. The story of her
conversion to God had already been related to her
companions by the blessed Elerius, but she appeared
now as if beginning her conversion over again. She
practised almost perpetual abstinence, continual
prayer, and humility of conversation. The other
maidens accepted her as a pattern of patience and
obedience, and made her their guide in all that
belonged to their salvation. Every element of honour
and virtue they found abundantly in her; and the
veneration for her was proportionately great. The
superior, and the mother of the holy confessor Elerius,
whose name was Theonia, loved her with deep affection, and followed her counsels as much as her own
or that of any of the other virgins in the care of the
house and its consecrated inmates. Often, when
speaking of her longing for the celestial kingdom, she
drew tears from the mother's eyes, and would weep

herself. Theonia was a woman of great authority and perfection in religion, wholly intent on works of charity and mercy; and, while she loved them all with a devotion not to be measured, she cherished the holy Winefride with glad affection and deep reverence, and did much to increase the veneration the others also bore her. St. Elerius, who served the Lord apart, with his brethren and fellow-disciples, in simplicity of heart and extraordinary affliction of spirit, sometimes came to visit her, and often spoke of her to others. Also, he often spoke to her of the secrets of Heaven and sometimes of the mysteries of the Church, and found in her a complete knowledge of all that belongs to God, as well as profound good sense and wisdom in all things belonging to the necessities of exterior life. All this could not long be concealed, and, in time, the convent where she dwelt obtained wide celebrity, and was held by all men in the highest reverence. The faithful people came in troops to see the maiden who had allowed her head to be cut off for the love of Christ, and had been restored to life at the prayer of a Saint, and they loudly proclaimed the place where she dwelt to be a highly honoured and holy spot. Some of them were satisfied with seeing and speaking of her, others humbly desired to be allowed to see the mark round her neck, and this request she did not like to refuse, for fear of checking their devotion, or being herself suspected of pride. They could not keep from tears when they saw the white scar on her skin, and would return home filled with admiration and praising God for His marvels.

CHAPTER IX.

Second Death at Gwytherin.

AFTER THE DEATH OF ST. THEONIA, ST. WINEFRIDE PRESIDES OVER THE CONVENT AT GWYTHERIN. HER PIOUS DEATH IN THAT HOUSE, AND BURIAL.

ONE day, the blessed Elerius entered the doors of the convent to speak to the holy virgin, Winefride, of the things of God, and their conversation turned upon the recollection of death. The Saint took the opportunity of saying something which he had often revolved in his mind. He said: " I rejoice that God sent you to this place to lay my body in the grave, and preserve my memory after my death. I have often asked of God to send one of his servants or handmaidens here to bury me and make this place famous after my time." The blessed maiden answered to this: " It will not be so, nor is this what God has appointed. You will, indeed, commit to the earth my lady, your mother, and I shall then be living and stand by your side ; then, and after a very few years, it will be your task to bury my body. Afterwards you will finish your course full of days, and being translated to your fathers, will find in the heavenly kingdom the treasures you have laid up on earth." The holy confessor withdrew, and very soon the prediction began to be fulfilled. The blessed Theonia was seized with mortal sickness, and perceived death to be approaching. Her daughters, the virgins who had lived under her

care, were profoundly affected at the approaching loss
of the mother who had trained them to God's service
and taught them the Divine mysteries. She consoled
them, saying that such lamentations might be reason-
able if a better was to be succeeded by a worse, and
the rights of God were endangered by an evil succession; but where to good better succeeds, and the
cause of God is in progress of advancement, they
should rather accept with spiritual joy the ameliora-
tion promised them. "You ought," she said, "to
bear my death patiently, since you will still have the
blessed Winefride, in whom you will find all that is
needed for instruction and example for your salvation.
Reverence her, imitate her, follow her as a guiding
star, cast upon her all your cares, not doubting that
she will be in all things your helper with God, She
received from the hands of her son, the holy Elerius,
the life-giving Communion of the Lord's Body and
Blood, and leaving this world, rendered up her spirit
into the hands of the holy angels.

On his mother's death, the holy man committed
the care of the convent to the blessed Winefride, who
accepted it only because she feared some judgment
of God if she refused. She carried her austerities,
and the sufferings she inflicted on herself, to the
utmost degree of endurance; but was always simple
and humble in habit, and in speech so beautiful and
attractive, that people of all ranks, even the highest,
from all parts of Wales came to be edified with her
conversation. Robbers and invaders of the property
of others were struck with compunction when they
saw her and heard her words, and some of them were
so far converted to God as to make public confession
of their crimes. No one ever spoke to her who was
not better and happier for doing so. The holy Elerius

often spoke of her publicly, declaring that God had appointed her for the illumination of their country, and that a virtue from on high dwelt in her. This, indeed, was the universal belief, and was attested by wonderful cures of the sick which followed her prayers. The infirm always left her healed, the sad went away rejoicing; cares and sorrows of mind, of body, of circumstances, all seemed banished by her presence, not to return. She was so withdrawn from the love of the world that she thought the smallest luxury admitted into the house a sort of pollution; while in the care of the maidens entrusted to her charge she omitted nothing that could contribute to their spiritual welfare, and in all things showed the profoundest wisdom and discretion.

And it was while the virgin Winefride, beloved of God, was thus devoting her life to the service of the Supreme Lord of Heaven and earth, that the Lord Jesus, willing to withdraw His faithful servant from the life of labour to eternal rest, made known to her the approaching hour of her departure. The communication was made to her while she was praying in the oratory at night. She received it with the deepest joy, and did not conceal her triumph and rejoicing. She continued to watch in prayer all night and labour in charity all day. She frequently spoke of her approaching end. Her companions grieved; St. Elerius, fully sensible of the loss he was about to suffer, yet exerted himself to give her every assistance and support in her preparation for the change which awaited her.

She was taken ill with a disorder of the bowels, which occasioned her acute pain. She prayed God to take charge of her, and not leave her soul a prey to the enemy; and, sending for Elerius, fortified herself

E

with the Viaticum of the Lord's Body and Blood.
Then, witnessing the grief of her companions, who
were in dismay at their approaching loss, she said to
them : " Grieve not for my departure, my daughters,
for God's mercy is removing me from present misery
to the good which is highest and unchangeable. I
rejoice now that I refused an earthly bridegroom,
that I despised the pleasures of the world, that I
determined to possess nothing of my own. I am
going to Him for Whom I forsook all things, and in
comparison of Whose love I counted all things earthly
as nothingness and filth. I shall behold Him for
ever, for Whose sake I threw away myself and all I
might have possessed. Do you embrace with diligent
devotion the same Lord, and keep yourselves for the
celestial Bridegroom, to Whom you are betrothed and
pledged. Only by His aid can you hope for safety,
when your own end comes, and escape the snares of
the enemy. All that carnal eyes are capable of looking upon, is slight and transitory. Care not for that
which is to-day, and to-morrow is not, nor ever turn
aside from the changeless good which cannot fail, in
which there is peace, and safety, and joy for ever."
Then, addressing herself to prayer, she laid down her
spirit, to be taken up into the hands of God.

She was taken ill on the first day of November,
and died on the second, having made it a request to
St. Elerius that she might be interred near the body
of his mother, St. Theonia.

St. Elerius took care to comply with this request,
and the body having been placed in the church, and
the offices of religion solemnly performed, it was
carried to the grave amid the lamentations of all the
bystanders. The cemetery in which she was laid
contains the graves of many saints and holy persons

of great merit, among them the holy confessors Chebius and Senanus, of whom the former was buried at her head, the latter in the same row. They were both celebrated men, and many churches are erected in that country in their honour, in which frequent miracles have been, and still are, wrought. The blessed Theonia rests on her left hand; the names of the other occupants of the graveyard are now only known to God. For, so many holy men and women are buried in that place, that it has been found impossible to retain their names, or even their number, in memory. Large numbers of pilgrims visited the grave of St. Winefride, and numerous miraculous cures were wrought by her intercession, so that it soon became a frequented place of pilgrimage. After a few years, the blessed Elerius departed this life, full of sanctity and religion. He was buried in the church which bears his name, which is illustrated, even to this day, by many miracles.

CHAPTER X.

Negotiations for removing her Body to Shrewsbury.

A MONK OF SHREWSBURY HAVING BEEN HEALED BY
INVOKING ST. WINEFRIDE, THE PRIOR ROBERT IS
SENT TO GWYTHERIN TO BRING THE BODY OF THE
VIRGIN TO SHREWSBURY, WITH THE CONSENT OF THE
BISHOP OF BANGOR AND THE PRINCE OF WALES.

MANY years after the blessed Winefride, effulgent
with innumerable virtues, travelled to the Kingdom
of Heaven, and in the reign of William, who was the
first of the Norman kings to succeed to the throne
of England, the Count Roger, a man of noble birth
and conspicuous for high character and piety, founded
a monastery in the city of Shrewsbury, placed an
abbot at the head of it, and collected there a number
of monks. In process of time this monastery, by
God's mercy, greatly increased, and spread the
fragrance of Divine sanctity among the inhabitants
of all that region. The brothers were sensible that
they were deficient in the possession of the relics of
saints, and, anxiously considering the question, they
concluded that in Wales, a country which in former
times had been hallowed and adorned by the presence
of so many holy men and women, they might expect
to find what they sought.

One of the brethren, about this time, was taken
alarmingly ill, and his condition occasioned the gravest
anxiety to all the community. They not only prayed

earnestly for his recovery, but sent round to all the
neighbouring monasteries to implore the prayers of
the brethren on his behalf; and, in compliance with
this request, the monks at Chester went in procession
to their church to intercede with God for his recovery.
While they were prostrate before the altar, devoutly
chanting the seven Psalms with this intention, one of
their number named Radulf, who filled the office of
sub-prior and was a man of great simplicity of mind,
fell asleep. In his sleep he saw a maiden of extraordinary beauty standing by him, who looked at him
with a gentle expression and said : " What is it that
you are on your knees praying for ? " He answered :
" A brother, who is one of our friends, is grievously
sick, and we are praying for his recovery." She
answered : " I know that the brother of whom you
speak is out of his mind. But, if you really wish for
his recovery, let one of you go to St. Winefride's Well
and say Mass in the chapel dedicated to her, and the
sick man will recover." So saying, she disappeared.
The monk awaking, and supposing what he had seen
to be only the illusion of a dream, said nothing about
it for forty days, during the whole of which time the
patient continued ill and kept his bed. Information
of this long duration of the malady at length reached
Chester, and the sub-prior then related his dream.
It was very favourably received by his associates,
who were already well aware of the great merits of
this holy virgin and the cures wrought by her intercession, and they had no difficulty in believing his
account and that it was the blessed Winefride herself
who had appeared to him. Accordingly, they sent
two monks to say Mass in the church by the fountain
of St. Winefride, and to pray for the sick man, who
recovered at the very hour the Mass was said, to the

great rejoicing of his companions. Shortly afterwards, the brother who had been sick proceeded to the same spot, to give thanks to God and the holy virgin for his recovery, and having prayed in the church, drank of the fountain and washed in it, returned in perfect health. From that time all the brethren cherished a great devotion to St. Winefride, and were anxious, if possible, to obtain a portion, even the least portion, of her relics; and knowing the difficulties that attended this enterprise, they earnestly and constantly besought God to grant them this favour.

At that time, King Henry,* a powerful prince and a friend of peace, directed the government of the kingdom, and tranquillity everywhere prevailed. Under these circumstances, the brethren were enabled to send messengers into Wales to inquire for the burying-places of several eminent saints, and especially the spot where St. Winefride reposed, which they particularly rejoiced to discover. They further obtained the consent of the Bishop of Bangor, and that of the principal chiefs and great men of Wales, for the removal of the relics. The death of King Henry, which occurred suddenly at this time (December 1135) and was followed by much political disturbance, compelled them for the present to defer their enterprise; but in the second year of Stephen, tranquillity being then in some degree restored, the Abbot of Shrewsbury, whose name was Herebert, by the counsel of the brethren, sent the Prior Robert into Wales, accompanied by another monk, whose name was Richard. The prior had previously been told, in answer to his inquiries, that if he would come himself he would obtain what he

* Henry I.

wished. He went first to the Bishop of Bangor, and was by him introduced to the prince of the land, by whom he was courteously received, and who, having heard the cause of his journey, said to him : " I do not think that you and your companions would have undertaken this toil and labour, if your design were not in accordance with the will of God and the wishes of this holy virgin. She may possibly feel that she is not regarded with due reverence by the people of her own country, and may wish to be carried elsewhere to receive the honours which her countrymen have neglected, or forgotten, to pay her. I therefore readily concede what you wish, for fear if I refuse I may suffer the effect of her indignation. And sinner as I am, stained with every iniquity, the last and worst of men, I would go boldly with you to the tomb, and deliver the sacred bones to you with my own hands if public business did not call me elsewhere. The pains you have taken, and the visions you have seen, indicate that it is her will and pleasure. Go, therefore, with my full permission and consent. You will find some who will oppose you, but you may confidently resist them, under the protection of her who has called you to your task. I will send a messenger to the place, to let them know my will, and endeavour to soften their hostility." Thus saying, he dismissed them in peace.

CHAPTER XI.

The finding of the Body.

ROBERT AND HIS COMPANIONS, ENCOURAGED BY VISIONS, ARRIVE AT GWYTHERIN, AND OBTAIN POSSESSION OF THE TREASURE.

LEAVING the presence of the Prince of Wales, they repaired at once to the place where the body of the venerable Winefride was laid. There were in all, seven; the prior already named, the Prior of Chester, a certain priest of the Welsh nation, a man of many high qualities, a brother whom the prior had brought with him from the convent, and three others. On their way they met a man of some consequence in that country, who stopped them, and asked which was the Prior of Shrewsbury, and being informed on this point, said to him: " I come to speak on behalf of the inhabitants of the manor which contains the bones of St. Winefride, to tell you that they are full of indignation at your project of removing the relics, under the protection of which themselves and every-thing belonging to them are placed; and I am to assure you that the anger of the prince, the threats of their own immediate lords, and offers of money, will all be unavailing to obtain their consent." Having said this, he went away. The prior and his companions, not knowing what to do, had recourse to Him Who stills the tempests of the seas, to appease the wrath of these opponents of their pious errand, and continued their route, animated with confidence in Divine assistance. Arriving near the cemetery, the prior sent on the Prior of Chester and the Welsh priest, who were known in the neighbourhood, to see what steps it would be best to take.

He himself remained that night in a village in the vicinity, the monk of his own convent being his companion, and passed the time in considerable anxiety on account of the message delivered to him during the day. When behold, after they had said matins, a woman of grave and noble aspect appeared to a certain man who attended on him, and said these words: " Rise at once, and tell your master to lay aside all sadness and anxiety, and raise his hopes to God, for he will leave this country in great joy. She for whose love and honour he came hither will further his wishes and obtain their fulfilment, and that soon. He will go back with joy, and rejoice his fellows with his coming." The prior himself was also favoured with a vision of the same import. A very holy abbot who formerly presided over the monastery at Shrewsbury, and died at an advanced age, and full of sanctity, by name Godfrey, appeared to him and soothed his anxiety, saying: " Be not faint-hearted, but have confidence, for by God's help we shall overcome our enemies, and obtain a victory over those who resist us. Be sure that we shall very soon secure that for which we so devoutly wish." So saying, he disappeared. These visions restored them to some measure of confidence and hope. They were recounting them in the morning, and deriving encouragement from what they heard and told, when one of their messengers arrived with an assurance that all was arranged, and they were

to follow him at once, for they would find that of
which they came in search, and might at once bear
it away. As soon as their prayers were said, they
mounted and rode to Gwytherin, where they called
up the priest of the village, to whom they gave a
private intimation of their errand, but told it to no
one else.

The priest listened patiently to what they had to
say, and answered as follows : " I am easily induced
to second your views, for in the first place I wish to
be more intimately associated with your monks and
clergy, and in the second place I have long since
been made aware of God's will, and that of our holy
virgin, on this subject, as I will briefly and truly
explain. I was watching in the church you see
there on Easter eve, ready to sing matins when the
hour arrived. Having duly recited the psalter, I lay
down to rest on the altar steps, when I saw a vision
which greatly terrified me, and warned me to offer
no resistance to your request. I was not, I thought,
as yet sound asleep, when a young man of extremely
splendid appearance, and with the aspect of an
angel, began to shake me, and said, ' Rise.' I thought
he was rousing me to say the office, and I answered,
' It is not yet time. I will not rise.' He went away,
and I sank into deeper sleep. A second time he
came, and shook me more violently than before,
and said, ' Rise, rise.' I would not obey him, and
repeated my former words, and covering my head
with my cloak, fell fast asleep. Soon afterwards he
came a third time, and very violently pulled away
the cloak from my head, and below my shoulders,
and said, ' Rise, rise, rise, and follow me.' I rose
hastily, in a dream as I found afterwards, and
followed his steps, till we came to the sepulchre of

the blessed virgin Winefride. He pointed this out
to me with his finger, and said: ‘Mark this spot
well, and remember what I say to you. If any one
comes this year, or next, desiring to remove this
stone,’ and he pointed to the gravestone which
covered the sacred remains, ‘take care to offer no
opposition. If he wants to remove the earth, let
him do so, and resist not. And if he wishes to carry
away the virgin’s bones, do not object, but aid him
in every way you can. If you refuse to obey my
words, and despise the admonition which is sent to
you from Heaven, you will soon be seized with a
long and painful malady, and so end your days.’
With these words the angelic vision, for so I consider
it, disappeared. I am therefore well disposed to
give you every assistance in your enterprise, and
help you all I can. You may count upon me. Call
the others and set them to work, and I will give you
every assistance in my power.

> Et quoniam vestris oculis sors obtulit illos,
> Dicite quæ vultis, quia sunt audire parati.” *

Then the prior, availing himself of the priest’s
assistance as his introducer and interpreter, addressed the people who were assembled, explaining
the reason of his journey, and soliciting their consent
to the object he had in view, with all the persuasion
he could use; telling them the whole story of the
visions, and of everything that had occurred from
the beginning, and protesting that he had undertaken
his errand in consequence of the suggestion and
admonition of the holy virgin herself. He had
almost convinced them, when a man who was

---

* These last words appear to be a poetical version of Acts x. 33, for
which we are indebted to the Welsh priest.

present, a son of Belial, rose suddenly, and threw
the whole assembly into confusion. He said it was
wrong to tear saints away from the soil of their
nativity, and carry them into foreign lands, and
angrily declared, as if he was possessed by furies,
that he would not permit it to be done. Some of his
party endeavoured to compose him, and desired the
others to go and consult the rest of the people, and
report their general sense and decision; and while
they were gone away for this purpose, the prior,
perceiving the mind of the man just mentioned to
be obstinate, and his temper malicious, and that he
was in truth the only obstacle to the realization of
their wishes, by the advice of the brethren, sent him
a sum of money, which had the effect of bringing
him over to our side, and he joined the consultation
as one of our advocates. The rest had yielded purely
for love of God, and seeing this man so suddenly
and completely converted, they were filled with
admiration, ascribing it to Divine influence, and
were the more encouraged to give way. After long
discussion, and the interchange of many embassies
between the parties, they all unanimously consented,
and the prior and his companions, giving thanks to
God, at length went to the spot they were in search
of.

The place which enshrined so great a treasure is
a cemetery, fenced off from that which is now in
use, filled with the bodies of numerous saints, and
reverenced so greatly by the inhabitants that no one
ever presumes to enter it except for prayer. In the
midst of the ground, and at the head of the grave
of St. Winefride, there stands a wooden oratory,
which is much frequented, and to which access is
always open, and many who are sick, infirm, or

diseased, go there for healing. Nor have they to
wait long for the succour they implore, for the merits
of the saints buried there send them away healed of
their complaints. No brute animal, of any species,
can enter that ground and live, for the moment they
begin to browse the grass which grows upon the
graves of the saints, they fall dead. Nor are human
intruders allowed to escape with impunity. Two
years before the visit of the brethren, one of the
inhabitants of the place had made himself a pair of
shoes of raw hide, and wanted a string to fasten
them. There is a large oak among the saints'
tombs, left for centuries untouched out of reverence
for the spot. The man in question went to this tree,
with the design of cutting off some of the fresh inner
bark, to manufacture what he wanted, and carrying
a hatchet in his hand. He raised the hatchet and
struck the tree, but to his astonishment the hatchet
adhered to the tree, and his right hand to the
hatchet, while the muscles of his arm stiffened, so
that he was absolutely incapable of moving it.
There he remained, till his cries for help summoned
a large concourse of the inhabitants to the spot, of
all ages and both sexes, but they could give him no
assistance, and could only weep and compassionate
him when he related what had occurred. They
advised him to make confession of his fault, express
his sorrow for his failure in reverence for the holy
tombs, and ask forgiveness. This he devoutly did,
while his parents and relatives knelt at the tomb
of St. Winefride, whose name was better known to
them than those of the other saints who were there
interred, and asked for mercy. When they all cried
out together, " Holy Winefride, have mercy on him,"
at once, by God's mercy, he drew away his hand,

and the hatchet fell to the ground. The spectators glorified God, and were much strengthened in their devotion to the holy virgin. The oak is still standing, bearing the mark of the blow of the hatchet, to attest the truth of this story. Owing to this and many other miracles which have taken place there, the spot is held in great veneration by the devotion of the people.

To this holy place the brethren were conducted, to take possession of the treasure they sought. The prior first, and led, as I think, by the Spirit of God, without any other guide to show him the way, went straight to the tomb of St. Winefride ; and standing at the head of the grave, and waiting for his companions, was assured, as if by an interior voice, that that was indeed her resting-place, and that they would there find what they desired to see. Those who were accompanying him to show him the place came up immediately afterwards, and told him the same thing. The people then retired, and the monks and priests having chanted some of the psalms, two brethren, namely, the Prior of Chester, and the monk from Shrewsbury, with the aid of some workmen armed with spades, dug up the ground. Not until they had laboured long, and were nearly exhausted with toil, was their patience rewarded. The bones were taken out of the dust, and wrapped in cloths, as well as time and opportunity would allow ; and having said farewell to the people of the place, they set out, greatly rejoicing, on their homeward route.

CHAPTER XII.

The Translation and Reception at Shrewsbury.

THE SACRED BODY IS CONVEYED, AMID STRIKING
MIRACLES, TO SHREWSBURY, AND PLACED WITH
GREAT SOLEMNITY IN THE CHURCH OF THE MON-
ASTERY.

PROCEEDING cheerfully along the road, they talked
of various subjects to beguile the way, and more
than one made the remark that he would count it
of more value than any treasures, if an opportunity
occurred of testing the genuineness and miraculous
virtues of the burden they carried. God soon
permitted them this satisfaction. They stopped to
rest in the evening at the house of a good christian
who offered them hospitality; and when they lay
down to sleep, a sick man in another part of the building began to groan and cry with pain. The prior
having inquired what was the matter, was told that
the patient was very ill indeed, and it would be a
great mercy of God if any means of his restoration
could be found. The prior asked for some water,
blessed it, put into it a few grains of dust from the
head of St. Winefride, and sent it to him to drink.
The invalid did so, and immediately lay down and
went to sleep; but in a very short time he awoke
and declared himself quite well, giving thanks to
God and the holy virgin for his recovery. The
messengers were greatly consoled by this event, as

a proof that they had been successful in their mission, and were strengthened in devotion to the holy maiden. Many other things occurred on the road which proved that they carried with them a sacred gift from Heaven.

On the seventh day they drew near the city of Shrewsbury, whence they had set out, and sent on to the monastery to announce their approach. The monks in chapter were delighted at this intelligence, and decided that the sacred relics should be deposited in the first instance in the church of St. Ægidius, at the entrance of the town, because a treasure of such great importance could not with propriety be introduced into the monastery except with the authority and blessing of the bishop, and assembly of the people of the province. The prior accordingly went to the bishop for his approval. The brethren in turn said the offices night and day devoutly in presence of the holy relics; and during the next few days all the inhabitants of the neighbouring country poured into the town, to avail themselves of the prayers and merits of the holy maiden. There was a young man in the town who was a cripple in all his limbs, to such a degree that his head bent almost to the ground, and he was unable to raise it. He had spent all he had in the world in experiments for his health, and he had now lost even the hope of ever being cured. Hearing of the arrival of the holy virgin, he asked some one to put him on a horse, which was done, and being held up on both sides, he was conducted to the church in which the relics were deposited. There he remained all night in prayer, and towards morning was sensible of acute pain in his joints. After that he slept a little while, and at dawn, when the priest began the office of Mass, he began to get better, though every one present expected he was going to die. After the Gospel, he went up to the altar with the others, to give his offering to God and the priest; then, having rendered devout thanks to God and the holy virgin, he walked back unassisted to his father's house.

This miracle inexpressibly delighted and rejoiced the people, and the news of it spread over all the country, urging the minds of all who heard it to the highest point of reverence and fear. The holy virgin's name was now in every mouth, and all eagerly inquired when the translation was to be completed. The prior returned from the bishop with his full authority, and God's blessing and his own to all who held the holy maiden in devout veneration. The day was fixed, and proclaimed in all the neighbouring churches, with an invitation for all to attend who wished to witness the august ceremony of the translation. This was duly carried out on the appointed day. The brothers went in procession to receive the relics, with the crosses and candles, and accompanied by an immense concourse of people, who all without exception bent their knees as the body of the blessed Winefride was carried by, and many wept for joy. There was a heavy shower of rain falling at the time all over the neighbouring country, and the brethren who had taken with them the precious ornaments of their church, which were of great value, were afraid that the solemnity might on this account be deprived of some of its external splendour. But their prayers to God, aided doubtless by the wishes of St. Winefride, relieved them of this fear by an evident miracle, for during the whole of the procession, from their first leaving the monastery until their return with the sacred relics, the waters

F

from the clouds were by Divine power suspended over the earth, and the drops of rain could be seen ready to descend, and yet by some heavenly power retained and held back. All who were present observed this phenomenon, and many thought a heavy shower was about to fall, and would disperse them. Others understood that the waters were held in by the power of God, for the greater honour of the holy virgin, and demonstration of her merit. The relics being received, and the procession about to return to the monastery, the prior, at the general wish, addressed the assembled people, on the graces and merits of the holy maid whose translation they were witnessing, and spoke at considerable length, and all the time the clouds were hanging in the sky around, threatening to precipitate their burden, and deluging all the country round with floods of water. The brethren took up the relics, with all due reverence, raising their voices on high in praise to God, conveyed them to the monastery, and laid them reverently upon the altar constructed in honour of the holy Apostles Peter and Paul. And there, in demonstration of the prerogative of this holy virgin, many sick are continually healed, and numberless miracles are done, to the praise of God; to Whom be honour, glory, and empire, for everlasting ages of ages. Amen.

THE MIRACULOUS WELL.

To face p. 8...

CHAPTER XIII

St. Winefride's Well and the Mission at Holywell.

THUS far the narrative of Robert of Shrewsbury, whose elegant and copious flow of language is necessarily very imperfectly represented in a translation. That he has somewhat amplified his materials, and has composed himself, in the earlier part of the foregoing narrative, some of the speeches he put into the mouths of the personages of his story, is of course evident; but its general outline, equally evident, is faithfully rendered as he received it from the mouths of those who handed it on to him. One of the most striking features of his history is its genuine piety, and the absorption of all the ideas and faculties of the writer in the one object of his life. The promotion of religion, the honour of the saints, the love of God, the celebration of His worship, and the fitting splendour of His temples—these things were plainly all this writer lived for, not professionally only, but sincerely and in real earnest. The Prior of Shrewsbury was a true monk and priest, not in position only, but in heart; and his associates appear to have resembled him. The monks of Chester go in procession to their church to pray for the sick brother at Shrewsbury; the Welsh priest lies down to sleep on the altar steps on Easter eve. And it suggests the question, what malignant power can have induced the English and British

peoples to forsake and persecute and drive away
these spiritual guides, whose whole aspiration was
for a better and more perfect world than this, and
whose lives were the pursuit and cultivation of all
that is lovely and of good report.

The relics of St. Winefride reposed in their resting-place in the conventual church at Shrewsbury
until the change of religion, when the monastery was
suppressed and confiscated by King Henry VIII.
During this time the convent was placed under her
protection, as well as that of the Apostles SS. Peter
and Paul. At the dissolution, the tomb of the Saint
was broken up, and the sacred relics dispersed. It
did not escape notice that a man who broke open the
coffin containing them, with a hatchet, broke his leg,
and died miserably; another who dug up the grave,
became paralyzed. One portion only, a finger, of the
body of Saint Winefride, escaped destruction, and
was in the possession, at the beginning of the last
century, of the Marchioness of Powys. This noble
lady presented it to Father Louis de Sabran, of the
Society of Jesus, who sent it to Rome; it was there
enclosed in a handsome casket, and preserved in
the English College. In 1852, the Rev. Albany
Christie, of the Society of Jesus, obtained one half
of it from Cardinal Asquini, Prefect of the Congregation of the Holy Relics, to send to England.
This was subsequently divided, and one portion is
now preserved in the Cathedral at Shrewsbury, the
other belongs to the mission at Holywell. There is
also preserved at Holywell a small slab of very hard
wood, about eight inches by four, which is traditionally
said to have formed part of the coffin in which the
Saint was originally interred at Gwytherin, but it
is not exhibited for devotion, the evidence of its

genuineness not being considered sufficiently trustworthy.

In 1093 the church at Holywell, and the sacred
fountain, were given by Adeliza, Countess of Chester,
to the monastery of St. Werburgh in that city; a
circumstance which apparently marks the progress
of the English conquests in Wales, as they were
effected gradually. In 1115, Richard Earl of Chester,
her son, went on pilgrimage to St. Winefride's Well.
In 1240, David, son of Llewellyn, Prince of Wales,
who recovered the independence of his country during
the troubled reign of Henry III., granted the church
of Holywell, with other extensive possessions, to
the monks of Basingwerk, who held it until 1537,
the year of the dissolution. Early in the fifteenth
century, and in the reign of Henry V., Pope
Martin V. granted certain indulgences to pilgrims
who visited the Well; and about the same time
Henry Chicheley, Archbishop of Canterbury, ordered
the festival of St. Winefride, as well as those of
St. David and St. Chad, to be observed throughout
the province. King Richard III. ordered the sum of
ten marks to be paid annually from the treasury for
the support of the chapel of St. Winefride, and the
stipend of the priest; and it was a few years later,
and probably before 1495, that the beautiful buildings
now surrounding the Well were erected, though they
were not completed at once, for among the armorial
bearings near the entrance is the shield of Catherine
of Arragon, bearing three pomegranates surmounted
by a royal crown. This princess landed in England
in 1501, as the bride of Prince Arthur, but did
not become Queen until her marriage with Henry
in 1509. The concourse of pilgrims to the Well
continued in the sixteenth century; and Thomas

Goldwell, Bishop of St. Asaph, who went into exile
at the accession of Elizabeth, and resided in Rome,
obtained from the pontiff the confirmation of the
indulgences granted by Martin V. In 1605 Sir
Everard Digby, the celebrated associate in the
"gunpowder plot," with his wife and two other
noble ladies, the Jesuit Fathers Garnett and Percy,
and a troop of thirty horsemen, went on pilgrimage
to St. Winefride's Well; and in the same year Father
Garnett succeeded in concealing himself there for
several days, from the active pursuit of the messengers
of the government sent to apprehend him.

The mission of the Society of Jesus at Holywell
was originated by Father John Bennett, or Price,
who resided there for thirty years, and kept the
catholic faith alive among the humbler classes of
the people, until in 1625, learning that the plague
had broken out with great virulence in London, he
hastened to the capital, though he was in the
seventy-fifth year of his age, to minister to the
sufferers, and in the exercise of this heroic charity
he was seized with the pestilence and died on
Christmas Day in the same year.

In the following year we find Sir John Bridgeman,
one of the judges, writing to the council to complain
of the affluence of pilgrims, of all orders and classes
of society, including many persons of position, to
the Well of St. Winefride. In 1629 we have a list,
from an unknown hand, of the pilgrims who attended
at the Well to celebrate the festival of the virgin
martyr. It contains the names of Lord William
Howard, Lord Shrewsbury, Sir Thomas Gerard,
Lady Falkland, and other names of well known
catholic families, but the whole number amounted
to fourteen or fifteen hundred, including a hundred

and fifty priests. Among these were six priests, all brothers, of the family of Latham of Mossborough.

In 1636 an attempt was made by the English Government, acting through Sir John Bridgeman, to prevent the access of pilgrims to the Well. There is an account of these proceedings, and what resulted from them, in a curious document preserved in the Royal Library at Brussels, a translation of which is here subjoined.

"A relation of the occurrences which took place at St. Winefride's Well, confirmed by the authority of Sir John Bridgeman, Knight, Chief Justice of Chester, in 1637.

" First, the aforesaid Sir John Bridgeman at the assizes of the county of Flint in April, 1637, issued an order to the churchwardens of the parish of St. Winefride to take away the iron posts around the fountain and disfigure the image of the Saint, close all the hostelries except two, examine all the pilgrims who came thither, and report their names at the next assize, and he sent this notice round to the magistrates of the county. On the authority of this mandate, and on the instigation of several malicious protestants, and especially one Rhys Jones, the churchwardens for that year, William Jones, brother of the above-named Rhys Jones, and like him a fierce protestant, and William Hughes, ordered the removal of the iron posts and rails, in opposition to the will of several persons of rank and authority in the county, and the general wish of the inhabitants of the town. William Hughes was disposed to listen to these remonstrances, but William Jones told him he would not consent to let them remain, though the whole town went bail for him. Rhys Jones vehemently urged his brother on, and stood by when the posts were removed, using many injurious expressions of the saints and in derogation of St. Winefride.

At the Michaelmas sessions in the same year the judge demanded an account of the execution of the order, and was informed that the posts had been removed * and the image whitewashed, but without producing much effect upon it. The inn-keepers refused to give the names of the pilgrims, on which account a fine was imposed upon them, and I believe, actually exacted.

"The judge died in January following of the ailment called Miserere, vomiting his excrements from his mouth for three days together.

"Rhys Jones lost the use of one side of his body at the time the posts were removed, and continued to languish till he died in February, though he was a strong man forty years of age.

"The house of William Jones was burnt to the ground on Wednesday in Holy Week. The origin of the fire was not known, but it was so active that the building, which was fifty or sixty feet in width, was burnt down in half an hour. His servants, at the time, were ploughing at a distance of two miles away, and the oxen stood still, and neither the driver or ploughman could induce them to move a step, so that they were obliged to unyoke them and lead them to the house, which they found burnt to the ground in their absence.

"All this is averred to be true by many grave and learned protestants, who were previously prejudiced

* The statue was afterwards removed and probably destroyed, but the richly carved canopy and niche were not defaced. In 1886 a very beautiful statue of St. Winefride was placed in this niche by the generosity of R. Sankey, Esq., J.P.—*Editor*.

against the saints, but now declare that they will never again meddle with the saints or anything belonging to them."

In the Annual Letters of the English Province of the Society of Jesus for 1642—43, it is related that several Catholics combined to bear the expense of building a large and fine house for the reception of the pilgrims to the Well, who were still numerous, and often included persons of rank. The house, when built, was to be entrusted to the Jesuit Fathers. But the design was interrupted by some catholics who were opposed to the Society, and represented to the magistrates that such a proceeding would give unnecessary offence to protestants. They even went so far as to say that the scheme was intended to develope into the foundation of a college of the Jesuits. The work was therefore stopped, but not until a hall of large dimensions had been built. At the assize in the same year the judge requested and obtained the use of this room to hold the court, and it did not escape notice that some of the persons who had so fiercely opposed the erection of the hospice were brought up at this assize, and sentenced to death.

The mission of the Fathers of the Society of Jesus in North Wales, the centre of which was at Holywell, was formerly constituted in 1670, having been previously subject to the college of St. Francis Xavier in South Wales. There was thenceforward a regular succession of superiors at the residence of St. Winefride, from 1670 to the suppression of the Society in 1773. King James II. made the pilgrimage to the Well in 1686, and on this occasion the king made over the chapel to the Fathers of the mission, it having previously been used as a court-room, or

for other secular uses.*   The queen presented the
sum of thirty pounds sterling for the adornment of
the chapel, and the king offered a garment which
had been worn by his illustrious ancestress, Queen
Mary of Scotland, on the day of her execution.   It
appears from the Annual Letters for this year that
the concourse of pilgrims increased greatly during
this reign, and was very numerous indeed, and from
all parts of England.   Many sick persons came for
healing, and some wonderful cures were effected.

At the outbreak of the revolution a tumultuous
mob broke into the chapel, and the priest's house,
both of which they dismantled, dragged the crucifix
by a rope round the feet through the streets, with
every insult and contumely, and burnt it in the
market-place.   The priest in charge, Father Roderic
Roberts, took refuge in the hills, where he was compelled to live among the woods and caves, with some
intervals, for two years.   The persecution only
gradually subsided during the next three reigns.

* It would appear from the following letter that it was the Queen,
Mary Beatrix, who gave the Well, or at any rate the chapel over the
Well, to the Fathers of the Society.   The letter is addressed to Sir
Roger Mostyn :

It having pleased the King, by his royal grant, to bestow upon me
the ancient chapel adjoining to St. Winefride's Well, these are to desire
you to give present possession in my name, of the said chapel to Mr.
Thomas Roberts, who will deliver this letter into your hands.   It being
also my intention to have the place decently repaired, and put to a good
use, I further desire that you will afford him your favour and protection,
that he may not be disturbed in the performance thereof.   You may
rest assured that what you do herein, according to my desire, shall be
very kindly remembered by

Your good friend,

MARY REGINA.

May 8, 1687, Whitehall.

Was it at this date that the stone bearing the device of the Society,
I.H.S. was built into the side of the wall which supports the pillars of
the chapel ?—*Editor.*

The confluence of pilgrims was discouraged, and though two or three Jesuit Fathers were usually resident at Holywell or in the neighbourhood, they were always liable to interference or annoyance. As late as 1718 the oratory was plundered by a band of men from Preston, led by an apostate priest named Hitchenor. Some of the Fathers nevertheless continued to reside at Holywell until the suppression of the Society, and after it, and of these, Father Edward Wright, who entered the Society in 1768, at the age of seventeen, and came to Holywell in 1777, lived to renew his vows at the restitution of the Order by Pope Pius VII., and died there in 1826, at the age of seventy-four. In 1870 a house was opened for the reception of poor pilgrims, during the summer months, by the exertions of the Rev. Maurice Mann, S.J., and placed under the care of the Sisters of Charity, who reside there and have a school for boarders, besides teaching the poor schools. This institution is supported by charity, and received the special blessing of Pope Pius IX., under his hand, dated December 23, 1871. The mission is now under the charge of the Rev. Thomas Swift, S.J. The attendance of pilgrims, and especially of sick people seeking relief, though it has very much fallen off in numbers compared with former days, has never wholly ceased, and is now on the increase, and the miraculous properties of the Well, when sought in faith, are still what they were, as will be seen from the evidence given hereafter.

CHAPTER XIV

Miracles recorded by earlier Biographers.

A SERIES of miracles extending over a period of more than twelve hundred years, is necessarily for the most part, as regards its details, buried in oblivion. The particulars of most of these occurrences are much alike in description, though differing in the variety of the numerous ailments, mental and physical, which flesh is heir to, and for which relief is sought; and the bulk of them only remain in the form of a comprehensive and traditional belief, deeply rooted in the mind of the people, and surviving the vicissitudes and prejudices of so many centuries. Such as have been recorded are collected in full detail in Father de Smedt's narrative, and we will proceed to give a somewhat briefer account of some of them here.

The monk of Basingwerk, to whom we are indebted for the earliest narrative of the life of St. Winefride, which has been translated above, appends to his Life a relation of several miracles which occurred at the Well in times then recent, and probably about the conclusion of the eleventh, or the earlier part of the twelfth century, and of the truth of which he must have satisfied himself.

During the wars between the Welsh and the Normans the country was much infested by bands of robbers. These desperate men sent a company of eight of their number to plunder the church of St. Winefride and the town of Holywell, which they did so effectually as to take away the beasts of burden which were tied up to the wall of the church. It was observed that this sacrilege did not remain unpunished, for in a very short time the eight met with violent and miserable ends, and the band who had despatched them were so entirely extirpated within a year that scarcely one of them survived.

A land-owner and warrior who was building a water-mill on the river, a little below the Well, made an attempt to move St. Beuno's Stone, and place it in the middle of his mill-pond, for what reason is not perfectly clear. He sent a hundred yoke of oxen for this purpose, with ropes, and all his workmen, and persisted in the attempt for some time, but without avail, for the stone remained immoveable. At last he struck it with his foot in a passion, but the nerves contracted and he remained lame all the rest of his life.

A rich man in the neighbourhood, who was fearfully crippled, so that his legs were bent double behind his back, and he was quite incapable of walking, had himself put upon a cart and driven to the chapel. There he made an offering to the holy virgin of everything he possessed in the world, rendering himself absolutely poor. He remained three days, bathed thrice in the fountain, and watched three nights in the church. On the third night all his bones cracked with a loud noise, and he found his limbs restored to their proper position and use, and returned home on foot.

A man who had been condemned to penance for his crimes had his hands bound together with iron chains, and carried them for many years, until his arms were dreadfully injured by the rust and friction of the chains. He came to the church, and having passed the night in prayer and watching, went in the morning to the fountain, and placed both his arms in the clear water. Then there appeared under the water two beautiful and delicate hands, which gently unfastened the chains, and set him free, and in no doubt to whom these kind hands belonged. He returned to the church to thank God, and left his chains hanging there for a memorial, and they remained many years.

A dropsical patient, brought with difficulty to the spot, after watching in the church, was healed at once by bathing in the miraculous water.

An epileptic patient, brought by his friends, was several times attacked by his dreadful malady during the few hours he remained near the Well. On one of these occasions he was outside the church when, feeling the fit approaching, he hurried in, and the priests prayed over him while the attack lasted. In the morning it came on again with renewed force. They took him up and threw him into the water, when he was completely cured, and had no return of the disease. This is only one out of a very large number of cures of epilepsy, a malady which would seem to have been frequent in former times, and for which the intercession of this holy virgin was believed to be peculiarly efficacious.

Another brought her child, who was dumb from his earliest years, watched with him in the church and then washed him in the fountain and poured some of the water into his mouth. The boy, who had never spoken before, immediately demanded his clothes and began to dress.

A band of young men, all more or less crippled and

deformed, came and bathed in the Well for cure. Only one of them, having more faith than the rest, was healed; and his joints, at the moment of his cure, suddenly cracked with so loud a report that it was heard at some distance. For the power of God, says the writer, cannot be hid.

A youth who was weak in his limbs, which seemed wasting away, as if dying before the rest of his body, earnestly called upon the aid of the holy virgin. She heard the prayer, and restored him to full health.

A man born blind came to the church, prayed in the customary manner, and went straight to the Well, where he washed and immediately received sight.

There are also related cures of patients so eaten by worms that they penetrated even to the marrow. Idiots and madmen, vexed by evil spirits, were brought, gnashing their teeth and talking language without sense, and bound in chains, but returned home free and under the direction of right reason. Patients suffering from fever, in all its forms, were healed at once by the application of the sacred water. There were cures innumerable of dropsy, paralysis, gout, melancholia, sciatica, cancer, alienation of mind, spitting of blood, obstinate cough, chronic pain and fluxion of the bowels, every known ailment that afflicts humanity, and to relate them all in detail would be impossible. Human suffering of every kind was sure of obtaining the compassionate aid of this gentle virgin, when sought with faith.

One evening a man came to the church, bringing with him the dead body of his little daughter for burial. The corpse, properly laid out and wrapped in funeral cloths for burial, was left alone in the church, during the night, and the doors carefully locked. The priest going into the church early in the morning, found the child released from the grave-cloths and moving about the floor on her hands and knees, too weak to walk upright, but otherwise perfectly well and asking to be taken into the house and to have some food.

Two clerks, at different times, stole books from the church of St. Winefride: a theft which was in those days of considerable consequence. One of them was caught in the act and beaten; for, as the writer observes, the workman is worthy of his hire. The other took his prize away, but found it impossible to sell it, and accordingly brought it back. He was suspended from his office. Both these instances of the detection and punishment of crime are regarded by the writer as miraculous in their character, and resulting from the resolution of the Saint not to permit any sacrilege in the spot consecrated to her memory.

Another series of miracles, probably of an earlier date, is given by Robert of Shrewsbury, at the conclusion of his Life of St. Winefride, and will be conveniently noticed here. He begins by saying that the wonderful revival of the holy maiden after her decapitation, and outbreak of the spring of water, occasioned (as might be expected) a great confluence of visitors to the spot from all the neighbouring country and all parts of North Wales, many of whom resorted thither in hope of obtaining cure for various ailments with which they were afflicted, and many wonderful cures were wrought. One of the earliest and most conspicuous of these was the case of a young girl, the daughter of a carpenter, blind from birth. Her father brought her to the church and, having first dipped her head in the fountain, she watched all night till morning. Then she asked to be allowed to sleep, and slept many hours. On waking, she found she could see perfectly, and having given thanks to God, went home with her father.

The northern part of Wales was, at one period, much infested by bands of robbers. Under these circumstances, the principal chiefs agreed to send a messenger round to all land-owners and house-holders who had any property of consequence to protect, to warn them to be on their defence and prepared for attack. This messenger, being pursued by the robbers, took refuge in the church of St. Winefride, which he entered, leaving his horse tied up at the church door. One of the robbers, more daring than his fellows, placed his hand inside the door, unloosened the end of the bridle, which was fastened there, and led the animal away. But very soon the arm with which he had committed this sacrilege began to give him such intolerable pain that he acknowledged he would rather die than endure it. At length, overcome by the agony he endured, he came to the church, confessed his crime, and implored the prayers of the holy virgin, after which his sufferings were sensibly relieved. He did public penance, and used all the influence he possessed with his former associates and all others to whom he spoke, to warn them of the danger of braving the anger of Almighty God and the indignation of St. Winefride.

On another occasion the robbers led away a cow, which they found on the lands belonging to the church. Not wishing to lead it along the roads, for fear its footprints should indicate which route they had taken, they made their way with their booty across some rocky ground, which they supposed would leave no trace of their passage. To their astonishment they found the footmarks of their four-footed companion were deeply imbedded in the solid rock, and could neither be erased nor concealed. They accordingly ran away and left the cow in a wood, where it was soon traced by its miraculous footprints and brought back. It was observed that it left no similar traces on the journey home. The robbers, fearing the vengeance of Heaven, came afterwards to the church, made public confession of the crime, and were allowed to depart.

Two young children afflicted with some congenital malady were thrown into the spring at its source, whether with a view of curing or drowning them is not clearly stated, but after they had been carried some little distance down the current, their mothers took them out of the water safe and sound, and healed of their complaints. It soon became established that the waters of the Well were an infallible cure, especially in cases of fever, and the number of such cases brought thither was very great. In many of these cases the patients were advised to have recourse to the waters by the virgin herself, who appeared to them in their dreams.

A water-mill, which stood on the banks of the river below the Well, and which belonged to the church lands, ceased working, either because the stream was swollen with melted snow, or from some other reason. While it stood idle some thieves stole all the working gear used for grinding flour, and sold these implements to another mill. But, when fitted in its new place, the machinery would not work, and came to a standstill. The new proprietors could not in any way explain this phenomenon; but, as it continued, they took the whole of their new purchase and threw it outside. The thieves took possession once more of the discarded implements, and sold them to another mill, and afterwards another, but everywhere with the same result. At last they took them back and replaced them where they had found them, and coming to the church made confession of their fault and did penance. The story was soon known all over North Wales, and greatly increased the respect and reverence of the common people towards St. Winefride. The writer adds that this reverence had not sensibly diminished down to his time, nor had the series of miracles ever ceased, confirming to the letter the truth of the promise given to the holy virgin by St. Beuno.

Only less signal and illustrious were the miracles of healing wrought at her tomb, in the burying-ground of Gwytherin, where the blind received sight, and the deaf hearing, and prayer was marvellously answered, to the glory and praise of God.

It is true that Robert of Shrewsbury does not absolutely vouch for, and cannot be expected to guarantee, the complete accuracy of every detail of the miracles he records. Most of them took place before his time, and rest upon local tradition and the general belief of the inhabitants of the country. But he considers them worthy of credit, and their truth is confirmed, as he observes, by the undoubted continuance of similar miraculous cures down to his time. It is further confirmed, as we proceed to show, by what has occurred, and that frequently, in times still more recent.

There are no miracles recorded in detail in the sixteenth century, beyond the general attestation of writers of the time, and the people who lived in the neighbourhood, that the series of miraculous cures did not cease, as appears from the statement of Bishop Goldwell, referred to above. But, in the seventeenth century, we have more detailed instances

of miraculous cure.   The first of these is the case of
the Rev. Father Edward Oldcorne, an illustrious
member of the Society of Jesus, who afterwards
suffered death for the catholic faith in the year 1606.
The circumstances are related by Father Mathias
Tanner, in his history of the martyrs of the Society.
He says that Father Oldcorne was so exhausted by
his apostolic labours, carried on in a time of severe
persecution, as well as by fasting, wearing hair-cloth,
the use of the discipline, long watching, and other
austerities, which he carried to an almost inconceiv-
able extent, that he burst a blood-vessel in his chest,
and constantly spit blood in alarming quantity, and
for this malady he could find no cure.   At last he
became so weak that he could scarcely stand upright,
and a gathering, having the symptoms of a gangrene,
formed itself in the roof of his mouth.   Having heard
of the fame of St. Winefride, and the miracles which
were wrought at the Well, he repaired thither and
said Mass in the church.   He was instantly and
effectually restored to health, using no other remedy
than the application of one of the crimson pebbles of
the Well to the ulcer in his mouth.

The Rev. Father Philip Leigh, or Layton, or
Metcalf, for he is known by all these names, resided
at the Well from 1700 till his death, at the age of
sixty-seven, in 1716, and during the latter part of
that time was superior of the residence.   He has left
a published account of the miracles which occurred
there in the previous century, within his own knowledge, and of which he had documentary proof on
which he could rely.   He observes that this limit
which he fixes, excluding everything not capable of
clear and satisfactory proof, tested by himself, has
induced him to omit any notice of earlier miracles,

because these rest on other testimony ; and he writes with the object of bringing conviction to the minds of protestants at a distance, who insisted in attributing the curative properties of the Well to the coldness of the water, or some other equally natural cause.

CHAPTER XV.

Miracles in the Seventeenth Century.

In the year 1606, Sir Roger Bodenham, a Knight of the Bath, was afflicted with a swelling in one of his feet, which subsided into a malady closely resembling leprosy. He consulted a Welsh physician, Doctor John David Rhese, who had studied his art at Siena and Padua, and having practised in many cities of Italy, had eventually settled in England. Dr. Rhese wrote a detailed account of the case, which puzzled his experience, and sent it to London by the hands of a Mr. Beale, Sir Roger's business agent, to be laid before the College of Physicians. That learned body replied that Dr. Rhese appeared thoroughly to understand the case, and had applied the right treatment, adding that the doctor was well known to them by reputation, and was a very learned man, with whom none of the physicians of London could presume to compare. If he could not effect a cure, the resources of the healing art must be despaired of. Dr. Rhese, who was a catholic, on this persuaded his patient to make the pilgrimage to St. Winefride's Well, and the journey of eighty-seven miles from his seat at Rotherwas, was with difficulty, but successfully, achieved. Sir Roger bathed in the sacred stream, from which he emerged completely cured, and his skin as sound as that of a newly-born infant ; nor did his malady ever return. He was converted to the catholic faith, and the circumstances of his cure were attested by many unimpeachable witnesses.

In December, 1637, Mrs. Jane Wakeman, wife of John Wakeman, of Rugeley, near Horsham, in the county of Sussex, was afflicted with an ulcer in the breasts, for which the physicians who attended her could find no hope of cure, except amputation, and they could give no assurance that even this dangerous and painful operation would relieve her, and might not even shorten her life. Under these circumstances, she made the long and fatiguing journey to Holywell, in dependence on the miraculous aid of St. Winefride. She left London in June, 1638, accompanied by her husband and his brother, Mr. Richard Wakeman, and Mr. Francis Nash. On reaching Beeley, in Worcestershire, she left all her dressings and bandages behind her, saying that she should want them no more. There was, at this time, a wide opening of the flesh, from which matter continually exuded in large quantities, as was seen by many women, both catholic and protestant. She remained only one night at the Well, and bathed three times. She received a complete and immediate cure and had no return of the complaint, nor did any trace of it remain except a slight scar. She lived five years after this, and bore three children, to whom she had no difficulty in giving nourishment in the usual way.

On a previous visit to Holywell, in 1630, this same Mr. Wakeman observed a man lying dead near the Well, and recognized him as a rascal who had jeered at and insulted him and other pilgrims, on the previous day, and spoken reproachfully of the Saint. An inquest was held on the body, and the jury—who were all, or nearly all, protestants—found that the deceased died by the just judgment of God, because he had spoken injuriously of that place.

About this time, in 1637, occurred the incident referred to above, when the image of the virgin was defaced and the iron rail on which the pilgrims leant when in the water, removed. It was observed that every person who was concerned in this sacrilege incurred some signal and unexpected calamity within a very short time.

In 1647, the wife of one John Clec, a gardener at Worcester, came on foot to Holywell for the recovery of her health, which was failing. Passing through Kidderminster, she stopped for some hours to rest at the house of a cousin, Antony Cooke, to whom she related the motives of her journey, and an account of many miraculous cures known to have been wrought by the waters of the Well. There was lying in an inner room a woman whose limbs had been crippled for six or seven years, and who was incapable of moving. She was a pauper supported in Mrs. Cooke's house at the expense of the parish, and, before Mrs. Clec went away, she sent her a message, urgently desiring to speak to her. She said she had overheard all that had been said about St. Winefride's Well, and gave her one penny, which was all she possessed in the world, imploring her, for the love of Christ, to give it in charity to some one at the Well, and pray for her recovery. This commission Mrs. Clec very gladly undertook, and punctually executed. She remained a week at Holywell, and passing Kidderminster again on her return, called on her cousin, at whose house she found the woman who had been sick, moving about actively and easily. On inquiry,

she learned that the patient had risen from her bed
strong and well, to the great astonishment of all who
knew her, on the day, and at the very hour, at which
she had bestowed the penny upon a beggar at Holywell.   This cure, at any rate, cannot be ascribed to
any chemical properties in the water of the Well.

Mrs. Mary Newman, wife of John Newman, who
was paymaster to Captain Jeremy Smith, at that
time in command of one of the British ships of war,
had been attacked in her childhood, and when not
more than five years old, with a fever so violent that
it entirely destroyed her strength, and she could not
stand, nor even put her foot to the ground.   This
continued until she was seventeen years of age.   By
that time the bones of her arms and legs were so dis-
torted, or dislocated, that those of the extremities
projected visibly upwards, above the higher ones.
Her father, having powerful friends, easily obtained
for her the advice of the court physicians, who, however, could hold out no hopes of cure, her malady
being beyond the reach of art.   She was touched by
the king, but no effect followed.   For many years in
succession she tried medicinal baths, in Somersetshire
(probably Bath) and elsewhere, but without effect,
and attempted to reach three in Scotland, of which,
however, she could be conveyed only to one.   She
was taken to France, bathed thrice in wine newly
pressed, and was touched by the hand of the most
Christian king at Paris, visited Sichem and other
holy places in Flanders; resided six weeks at Aix-la-
Chapelle; consulted, in Holland, the opinion of an
Italian prince, who had an extraordinary reputation
for medical skill; finally, was taken to Portugal, to
try the effect of some baths in that country; the
expense of all these journeys being defrayed by the

king, or the queen, of England. Among other expeditions in search of health, she had twice visited the Well of St. Winefride; but she had an ardent desire to go there for a third time, insomuch that she thought of it continually by day, and dreamed of it by night. She accordingly left London towards the end of May, 1666, and reached Holywell on the 6th of June, being the Friday after Pentecost. Immediately on entering the water she felt her limbs adjusted in their places, as if by some violent force, and with the assistance of some other pilgrims to the Well, was able to stand, which she had not done for eighteen years, and even to walk a few steps. On the feast of the Holy Trinity she bathed thrice, after which she was able to walk without assistance. All the witnesses of this miracle, who were numerous, made a formal attestation of the circumstance in presence of two persons of consequence, John Hughes of Combes, and Robert Price of Alwyducha. Here, again, a medicinal property in the water would hardly account for cure on a third visit, when they had already twice been ineffectual. The lady had, no doubt, heard of St. Beuno's prediction, and resolved to try the experiment a third time.

In the same year, 1666, on the 4th of April, at five o'clock in the afternoon, a boy named Hugh Williams, eight years of age, son of a farmer at Whitford, in Flintshire, and well-grown for his years, was playing with one of his school-fellows near a mill, not far from the Well, when he attempted to jump across the stream. He fell short, and was plunged into the water about three yards above the great water-wheel, which was revolving with full rapidity. His companion gave him up for lost, for there was scarcely two inches between the wheel and the bottom of the

stream, and the current, which was very strong,
would necessarily carry him directly under it. A
strong man, under such circumstances, could not
escape being crushed to death. The other boy, unable
to help him, raised a great cry of terror, which summoned to the spot all the school-boys, fifty in number,
who were in the school close by, the miller, and every
one else within hearing. Just then, a man named
William Bowen, who was fishing above the mill, saw
the child come out of the water and climb up the
bank, complaining that he had lost his shoes. He
was taken into the nearest house and examined by a
surgeon, but was found to have sustained no injury
whatever, with the exception of a slight abrasion of
the skin of one of his ankle bones. No one who knew
the spot could help saying that the child's life had
been saved by an evident miracle.

Cornelius Nicholas, of Tremaine, in the county of
Cardigan, two miles from the town of that name,
seventeen years of age, having lost both his parents,
went with his aunt into the service of a family in
that place. On December 21, 1673, towards evening,
he was suddenly taken ill, with an attack of faintness,
and such violent pain in his legs and feet that he
could neither walk nor stand. The surgeons who
came to see him applied various plasters and oint-
ments, and at last cut the limbs down to the bone
with knife and lancet. This treatment was continued
till Easter, without any improvement in the condition
of the patient, who, on the contrary, gradually grew
worse. Under these circumstances it was determined
to send him, if possible, to St. Winefride's Well; the
difficulty being the expense, as he was destitute, and
all his friends quite poor. They laid the youth on
a stretcher, and took him to the next village, trusting

to the charity of the country people to forward him
from village to village to his destination, and keep
him on the way. To the honour of the Welsh
people, and as a remarkable proof of their confidence
in St. Winefride, this was done, and the journey of
ninety miles successfully accomplished. He was
brought to the Well on the 11th of June, and the
next day, the Friday after Pentecost, plunged into
the water. The cure, to the great joy of his companions and all who witnessed it, was instantaneous
and complete, and the health, thus restored to him,
remained unimpaired for many years.

Roger Whetstone was a tailor at Sidmore, near
Bromsgrove in Worcestershire, was brought up a
Quaker, and continued in that sect to the age of
sixty years. He was then seized with a dreadful
illness which so greatly reduced his strength that he
was unable even to move his hand to his mouth to
feed himself, and in this condition he remained for
seventeen weeks. He recovered so far as to be able
to walk on crutches, but was quite unable to do any
work, and was reduced to beg his bread from door
to door. Hearing of the cures effected at St. Winefride's Well, he resolved, doubtless under the influence
of some good impression on his mind, to seek God's
help by going thither, and accordingly made the
journey on foot, and on his crutches, accompanied
by his daughter, a little girl eleven years of age.
He reached Holywell at mid-day on August 28,
1667. He could not be induced to bathe in the
fountain, a proceeding which seemed to him to
savour of papistry and superstition; but he sat down
at the head of the Well and drank a cup of water.
He immediately fell into an ecstasy, and then asked
for another cup of water, which he drank off. He

threw his crutches away, as far as he could, rose, and declared himself completely cured, and at once walked all round the Well, shedding tears of joy for his recovered strength. He was shortly afterwards received into the Catholic Church, and baptized together with his daughter, to whom some of the principal people of the county gladly offered to stand sponsors.

There is extant a remarkable attestation of the truth of the preceding narrative in the form of a certificate from Robert Hill, collector of the poor-rate at Bromsgrove, who declares that he was well acquainted with the above-named Roger Whetstone, and could testify that he was for three years so infirm that he could not walk without crutches, and at one time could not raise his food to his lips. He then gives the particulars of his cure, as above related, and adds: "This man, whom I often encountered at my own door, begging for alms, has been perfectly well ever since his return from Holywell, and now works at his trade, a fact well known, and not a little astonishing, to the people of Bromsgrove, many of whom, being out of health, followed his example and went to Holywell, and have declared themselves much better on their return. In witness whereof I subscribe this on October 2, 1667,—ROBERT HILL." Mr. Hill, who lived and died a staunch member of the Society of Friends, adds that his own daughter, fourteen years of age, recovered from sickness as soon as she took no other medicine than the water brought to her from Holywell.

CHAPTER XVI.

More recent Miracles.

THERE are only two miracles on record in the eighteenth century. In June, 1721, a woman named Catherine Harket from Rockliff in Cumberland, came to the Well riding on a donkey, and accompanied by her sister Mary, who was obliged to assist her in mounting and dismounting. The sick woman, being cured, sold the ass, and went away on foot rejoicing. In the following year, a man came from Edinburgh on crutches, and on his cure left his crutches hanging to one of the pillars of the Well, but they were stolen a month afterwards. These two cases rest on the authority of a torn letter, of which the signature is lost, but which is addressed to Mr. Heigham, in Drury Lane, and dated Holywell, June 23, 1733, and is now in the possession of his Eminence the Cardinal Archbishop of Westminster. Both the persons referred to were protestants.

In the early part of the present century there were two other cases which, owing to the circumstances attending them, obtained great notoriety, and were subjected to searching scrutiny. A girl named Winefride White, of good character, sound mind, and ordinary understanding and sense, had lived for seven years in domestic service in the house of a Mrs. Withenbury, at Wolverhampton. At the end

of that time she was taken violently ill with acute
pain in her left side, which spreading over the whole
of that side of her body, made her incapable of
moving. The pain extended to the back as far as
the spine, and she was so far paralyzed that if she
attempted to walk she had to drag her left leg after
her, as she could not support herself on it. This
was followed by a pain in the head so acute, and so
continual, that she could get no rest, and began to
fear her mind was going. The pain gradually
subsided, but left her so weak that she could scarcely
move any of her limbs, and if she tried to walk, with
a stick, was obliged to draw her left side with her,
as if that portion of her body was actually dead.
This illness lasted three years. Her mistress
charitably kept her in the house, and did all that
could be done to relieve her sufferings. She was
attended by the two most eminent medical advisers
in the town, Dr. Underhill and Mr. Stubbs, both of
whom ended by informing her that their art could
give her no relief, and that her disease was incurable.

Under these circumstances she resolved to have
recourse to the aid of Almighty God, and having heard
that many persons had obtained relief through the
prayers of the Blessed Virgin Mary, and of St. Winefride, at Holywell in Flintshire, she had a great desire
to go thither. It may be observed that the knowledge
of this fact, in a person of her condition of life, is
a proof of the persistence of the tradition among the
common people, because she could not at that period
have learned it from books. At the same time,
considering that her sickness might have been sent
to her for the good of her soul, she was anxious not
to take any step which might endanger her salvation,
and she therefore consulted the Rev. Mr. Walsh, her

protestant spiritual adviser, who heard what she had to say, and decidedly approved of her making the journey to Holywell, if she could find the means to do so. She set off, accordingly, on June 25, 1805, by the public coach from Wolverhampton, reached Shrewsbury the same day, and proceeded in a similar manner on the next day to Chester. Thence she went on, the same day, in a cart belonging to a Mr. Price of Holywell, who was returning home, and whom she luckily encountered just as he was starting. In this manner she reached Holywell on the morning of the 27th, but suffered so much on the journey that she began to think her mistress had been right in telling her, when she set out, that she never expected to see her come back.

At seven o'clock the next morning, after saying her prayers, she left the house of Mrs. Humphreys, in Well Street, where she had passed the night, and with great difficulty dragged herself to the Well, accompanied by Mrs. Midghall and two ladies named Bromley, who had arrived the day before from Liverpool. One of them kindly assisted her to descend into the Well. Dipping under the water, her mind was so overcome by the wonder of the whole occurrence, and a certain force that seemed to overmaster her, that she could not collect her thoughts until she found herself changing her bathing dress in the chamber of Mrs. Needham, the attendant at the Well. But she then discovered that she could stand; that her left leg was as strong as the right; that the pain in her back was gone; that her weakness had left her; that she was in every respect perfectly well. She remained a fortnight at Holywell, able to walk, run, or work, as well as any one. She bathed two or three times more, rather out of

compliance with custom than any further need of
cure, for she was cured completely at the first immersion. She then went to visit some friends at
Puddington in Cheshire, and afterwards spent a few
days with some other friends at Chester, and returned
to Wolverhampton, as she came, after an absence
of exactly a month. She was quite well, and able
to resume work, and never had any return of her
malady. She could easily walk six miles at a time,
and bore a weight of a hundred pounds on her left
side.

This extraordinary cure occasioned, as might be
expected, considerable wonder and comment in
Wolverhampton, where everyone heard of it, and
gave rise to no little controversy. Information of it
soon reached the Right Rev. John Milner, the Vicar-
Apostolic, to whom the central district of England
was confided, and recognizing the importance of the
case, he resolved to subject it to a close examination,
which the courtesy of the parties cognizant of it,
though they were all protestants, enabled him to
carry out. He went to Wolverhampton in the same
year, and took down the statement of Winefride
White in her own words, very much as has been
given above, to which she put her name. Mr. Stubbs,
the surgeon, gave him a full and extremely interesting
statement of the case in writing, adding the expression
of his opinion that the cure was absolutely unaccount-
able from natural causes. The bishop obtained also
a written statement from Mrs. Withenbery, fully
bearing out all the particulars as stated; and subsequently another to the same effect from Dr. Underhill, who had removed to Manchester. Then he
obtained the statement of Mrs. Midghall, who witnessed the cure, and who adds that immediately

after it Winefride walked with her to Greenfield
Abbey, a distance of two miles, and back, and in the
course of the walk ran rapidly down a hill, to show
that she had the full use of her limbs. Both the
Misses Bromley gave similar testimony, and put
their hands to it for its better publication. Then
the indefatigable bishop travelled to Puddington
and Chester, where he introduced himself to the
persons who had seen Winefride soon after her
restoration, and who assured him of her being at
that time in perfect health. This is certified by
Mr. Thomas Weld and the Rev. Mr. Ralph Platt,
at Puddington, and by the Rev. Mr. Penswick at
Chester. Returning to Holywell, he found that
Mr. Price, who was the landlord of the White Horse
in that town, was dead, but his widow perfectly
remembered all the circumstances, and assured him
that Winefride, on her arrival in Mr. Price's cart,
was so feeble that she could not ascend the stairs
without assistance, and when she saw her next day,
strong and well, she could not at first believe it was
the same person. She was satisfied of the reality
of the restoration, for Winefride came and took tea
with her on the following Saturday evening. Mrs.
Humphreys, at whose house of entertainment Winefride stayed, testifies to the same effect, and one
Robert Clubb, who met her at that house; as do
also Mrs. Needham, the keeper of the Well, Maria
Needham, John Hughes, the Rev. Edward Wright,
the protestant minister at Holywell, and Elizabeth
Jones. As the bishop points out, any idea of mysti-
fication or collusion among witnesses living at
Chester, Holywell, Liverpool, Manchester, Wolverhampton, and other places, and unacquainted for the
most part with one another, is out of the question.

H

All these certificates, and a complete statement of the case, were collected by the bishop, and published by him, under the title of "Authentic documents relative to the miraculous cure of Winefride White, of Wolverhampton, at St. Winefride's Well, *alias* Holywell, in Flintshire, on June 28, 1805; with observations thereon. By the R.R. J. M." A third edition of this pamphlet was published in 1806. It is given almost entire in the *Acta Sanctorum*, and it is to be regretted that the limits of our space do not admit of our reproducing it in full. The abstract just given will, however, convey a sufficient idea of the outlines of the case.

In the year 1859, there occurred at Holywell a remarkable instance of cure of blindness, in the case of a military pensioner named Christopher Clark, which excited so much attention that Viscount Feilding, now Earl of Denbigh, who was at that time the High Sheriff of Flintshire, took particular pains to investigate it. The results of this investigation, preserved in writing at Holywell, are also given at full length in the *Acta*. Christopher Clark enlisted in the 8th Regiment of Foot, when he was under sixteen years of age, and about the year 1810. In 1816 he was discharged on account of the weakness of his eyesight, but without pension; but seven years later, having by that time entirely lost his sight, he applied for a pension on the return of his regiment from Corfu. He was examined before a committee at Chelsea, by Mr. Clerk, a military surgeon, who pronounced him totally blind, and placed on the pension list, September 5, 1827. He was allowed one shilling and ninepence a day, being sixpence more than the sum usually given to discharged soldiers, because he pleaded that being

blind he required the services of a boy to lead him
about. After the lapse of thirteen years, on a
requisition of the military authorities, he underwent
another examination, from a surgeon of the 7th
Regiment at Clones, in the county Monaghan, in
Ireland, who pronounced him to be still blind. After
that a form was sent regularly every year to the
magistrates in Manchester, where he lived, which
they filled up and signed, certifying that Christopher
Clark continued to be blind, and that they had
satisfied themselves of this fact by bringing him up
before them and personally examining him. On
November 1, 1859, Christopher Clark came to
Holywell, and having fallen on his knees and
devoutly implored the aid of Almighty God and the
holy virgin, washed his eyes in the water, and found
that he saw light. After wiping his eyes, which
were flooded with tears, he could distinguish the
colours of his daughter's handkerchief, his son's
necktie, and other objects, and his eyes becoming
accustomed to their restored use, he soon saw as
well as he did before he ever lost his sight, and
indeed better. All these particulars were taken
down in writing on the 10th of the same month in
presence of several magistrates of the county of
Flint, and other persons, at Downing, Holywell,
and are signed by the mark of Christopher Clark,
by the Earl of Denbigh (Lord Feilding's father),
Lady Feilding, and another magistrate, as witnesses,
and they add that Christopher plainly proved in
their presence that he could see, for he read some
words before them from a printed book, and told the
time accurately from a watch. Further evidence
was obtained from one Anne Timlin, daughter of a
stable-keeper in Holywell, who saw Christopher on

his arrival, led by his guide, and subsequently heard
from him the narrative of his recovery. Major
Ready, staff-officer of the First Division in Manchester, also testified, in reply to Lord Feilding's
inquiries, that Christopher Clark was unquestionably
blind, and had received his pension for some years
from his, Major Ready's, hands ; and that he believed
him to be an honest man. The superintendent of
police at Manchester certified that Christopher had
lived six years at Woolley Bridge, near that city,
had a wife and children, and drew a pension, and
was almost entirely, he adds not entirely, blind.
Official evidence regarding the pension is furnished
by Mr. Monhead, the Secretary and Registrar of
Chelsea Hospital. Lord Feilding discovered in the
course of his investigation that there certainly were
some persons in Manchester who did not believe
Clark to be blind, among them a sergeant of police
named Wyld, and this gave rise to some curious
correspondence. Mr. Wyld says that Clark frequently
went unattended to a public-house near his own
residence, and returned ; and that when he passed
him in the street he had seen Clark turn round and
look after him. But both these circumstances admit
of explanation. A blind man soon learns the immediate neighbourhood of his own residence ; and
an old soldier, hearing the drilled footstep of another
soldier pass him in the street, would be not unlikely
to turn and look in the direction it had gone, even
though he could not see. The evidence in favour
of his blindness greatly preponderates, and the truth
seems to be that he had become so accustomed to it,
as not to exhibit any indications of his malady, as
is the case with some blind men, except to close
observers. And as Father de Smedt very reason-

ably says, on the supposition that his blindness was feigned, or exaggerated, he had no conceivable motive for pretending to be cured, inasmuch as his recovery cost him his pension.

The particulars of several other miraculous cures of a still more recent date are kept on record by the Fathers of the mission at Holywell. A few of these only, and the more remarkable, are related in the work of Father de Smedt. On July 6, 1859, a workman from Liverpool, named John Fitzgerald, whose ankle had been dislocated by the fall of a bar of iron while he was rolling a bale of cotton in Huskisson's dock, came to Holywell. He could only walk on crutches, and was quite disabled from work, for though the limb had been set by Evan Thomas, the ankle was painfully swollen. He bathed thrice in the Well, and the third time, kneeling on St. Beuno's Stone, prayed earnestly to God and St. Winefride for healing. He rose and left the Well completely cured, leaving his crutches behind him.

On the 3rd of August in the same year, Margaret Browland, sixteen years of age, who had lost the use of her right eye, was conducted to the Well, and standing on St. Beuno's Stone, joining her hands, and with her forehead on the edge of the Well, prayed earnestly to God, the Blessed Virgin, and St. Winefride. She recovered the use of her eye immediately. Her statement to this effect was made and signed in the presence of the Rev. Father Mann, then in charge of the mission.

John Ryan, born at Thurles, in Tipperary, sixty-six years of age, had worked for three years as stone-mason at Hartlepool. A splinter of stone which he was chipping struck him on the left eye, and the

inflammation which ensued affected his other eye
also. He attended the eye infirmary at Newcastle-
on-Tyne as an out-patient, and the surgeon in whose
charge he was placed, Mr. John Fife, said that in
twenty years' experience he had never seen a more
serious case. Eight blisters and five leeches were
applied, and lotions for the eyes prescribed, but
without effect. Ryan was afterwards for three weeks
under the care of Dr. Down, at Rotherham, but
derived no benefit. Then he went to Hull, and was
eleven weeks under the charge of Dr. Brown, one of
the physicians of the hospital for treatment of
diseases of the eye in that town, whose experience
was equally unavailing. At last he came to Holywell, on February 4, 1864, six months after the
accident occurred, accompanied by his wife. He
washed his eyes in the water for the first time on a
Friday, when he felt them burn, again on Saturday,
for the third time on the Monday following, after
which he could tell how many panes of glass there
were in St. Winefride's window, in the building over
the Well. On Wednesday, which was Ash Wednesday, he could see better and more clearly. All these
particulars are stated as they were related to Father
Mann.

Laurence Maher had been for four months under
treatment from Dr. Bickersteth, Physician of the
Northern Hospital in Liverpool, and Mr. Evan
Thomas, for acute pain in his right hand. He came
to Holywell on August 1, 1859, and after praying in the
chapel went to the Well and placed his hand in the
water, when a bone immediately fell from it. He
came back on the 15th, and placed his hand on
St. Beuno's Stone, when another bone, six inches in
length, fell out of it. His hand was soon restored to

its use. The authority for this statement is a certificate signed by himself.

In September, 1862, a pupil in the convent of St. Margaret, at Edinburgh, who had heard of the wonderful cures effected by the water of St. Winefride's Well, and who was suffering from acute pain in the knee which prevented her sleeping, applied to it some water which had been brought thence, and was kept in the house. This she did, in simple faith, one night when she was going to bed. She fell at once into a sound sleep, and woke cured. Father Mann adds to this that he received numerous letters giving similar accounts to this, but was not always at liberty to publish the names and circumstances.

Anne Murray, 6, Kaye Street, Middlesbury, Stockton-on-Tees, suffered severely from dropsy for two years. She spent thirty-two pounds sterling on remedies for her complaint, and was tapped eleven times, in which operations she lost a hundred quarts of water. She came to regard the operation with great dread and horror, and despairing of cure by ordinary means, came to Holywell, where, being too weak to enter the water, she washed herself thrice, standing on one of the steps. She took away with her some water and moss, a bundle of which she always wore. She came back on August 4, 1864, to return thanks for complete recovery.

Emma Fletcher, a young lady residing at Wigan, furnishes a statement of her own case, signed by her hand, and dated on the feast of St. Nicolas (Dec. 6), 1871. She says that she was first taken ill, apparently with violent neuralgia or contraction of the nerves, on December 13, 1865, and had a similar attack on the 25th of January following. On the 30th of June, having on that day sustained five-and-twenty seizures, she received Extreme Unction. From the 8th of July and onward they became more frequent, occurring three or more times, sometimes fifteen, and once eighteen times daily. This continued until September of the following year. She took to her bed, and on the 2nd of November again received Extreme Unction. Eight leeches were applied to her temples, and a blister kept open in her back, and renewed every two days. On July 4, 1868, she left home on a visit, but continued constantly ill. In July, 1869, an opportunity was afforded her of visiting Holywell, and on the 6th of July she bathed in St. Winefride's Well. She has never had from that time any renewal of her malady. The only respite she had previously had, during three years, was on the two occasions when she received Extreme Unction, and then she remained free from pain for one week. She had been under the charge of four physicians of eminence and three surgeons.

Mrs. Julia Hammond, St. Mary's Lodge, Croom's Hill, Greenwich, suffered for ten years from pains in the stomach, which attacked her after a confinement, and were so acute that for the greater part of that time she could neither walk nor stand. She arrived at Holywell on September 5, 1872, and the following day was conveyed in a carriage to the Well, and after some little hesitation entered the water, from which she emerged perfectly cured, sent away the carriage, and walked back to her hotel, the King's Head, in the High Street, to the great surprise and admiration of the people of the town. She walked the same day four miles to Mostyn, and visited Rhyl, Conway, and other places of note in the vicinity, before returning to London. These particulars are certified by the Rev. George Kammer-locher, of the Society of Jesus, who was in charge of the Holywell mission from 1878—1883.

A son of Mr. Lucas, 29, Wellington Street, Wigan, eleven years of age, fell from a crane twenty feet high, and injuring his head, became deaf and dumb. His father brought him to Holywell, and on his second immersion in the Well he recovered speech and hearing. This case occasioned great interest, and the inn was crowded with visitors anxious to satisfy themselves of the reality of the cure. It occurred in August, 1875. Three years afterwards a Mr. Walmesley, being at Wigan, called to inquire after him, and saw his mother, who declared that he had been perfectly well ever since.

Susanna Iles, of Kempsford, near Fairford, in Gloucestershire, suffered from 1872 to 1877 a linger-ing illness, which rendered her almost entirely unable to leave her bed, and almost equally unable to take any food, and quite incapacitated her for any active exertion. Medical advice could find no remedy for this complaint, and in time she left off taking any; nor could scientific men explain the cause of it. She arrived at Holywell in August, 1877, and was at once completely cured. The particulars of this case, which are very curious, are given at length in Father de Smedt's narrative, and confirmed by a letter from her father, written in the month follow-ing, and another from the medical man who attended her in her illness.

Louisa Jane Walker, a pew-opener or official at the Wesleyan Chapel, in Jetlow Street, Walton Road, Liverpool, who suffered from a malady which affected her voice, and had erysipelas in the knee, writes to return thanks to God and St. Winefride for her cure, which was effected by bathing once in the Well, and refers to two medical men in Liverpool, Messrs. Steward, Netherfield Road, and Bickersteth, Rodney Street, to confirm her statement.

George Sydney Doran, a pupil of the college of St. Francis Xavier at Liverpool, thirteen years of age, was taken ill on Saturday, February 1, 1879, with congestion of the brain, followed by paralysis, and became quite helpless, so that he had to be dressed and undressed like an infant. He was brought to Holywell in August, and on the 1st of September, having received Holy Communion from the hands of Father Kammerlocher, bathed in the Well. In the evening he complained of severe pain in his limbs, but the following morning he was quite well, rose and dressed himself, went up and downstairs, and could walk without difficulty, although on account of some nervous feeling for some time he carried a little stick in each hand to steady himself. These, however, he afterwards left off. These particulars are certified by four medical men in Liverpool and New Brighton.

Christian Rourke, Bogne Street, Dublin, writes about the same time that one day, some eight years before, he had come home to dinner, when he learned that his sister, who kept his house, had been called away, with other women, to attend a neighbour, a Mrs. Cunningham, who had been suddenly taken ill with a fit of such violence that it required the exertions of five women to hold her in her bed, and her cries were so loud that they could be heard at a great distance. Mr. Rourke had in his house some water from St. Winefride's Well, and obtained the consent of Mrs. Cunningham's father and husband to try the effect of it. The sick woman herself was unable to speak, but she nodded assent, and he administered a teaspoonful, three times, in the Name of the Father, and of the Son, and of the Holy Ghost. The woman then put out her hand, took the cup and drank off the contents. She became calm immediately, pronounced herself quite well, and had remained so ever since. Mr. Rourke adds that he had given the same water to several persons afflicted with bad eyes, and so far as he knew they were cured in every case.

Mary Keighley, 76, Hagley Road, Birmingham, suffered from a disease in one of her legs, so severe that she declares no words could describe the pain she endured, and her medical adviser told her that her case was hopeless, and she must expect to be a prisoner to her couch for life. She received some water from the Well, given her by a Miss Morris, servant to Mrs. Lemkey, and at the first application the pain entirely ceased. She continued to use it for a week, until three sores in her leg were healed. Her wonderful cure, she adds, had occasioned great admiration among her protestant friends.

William Radekin, born at Oldham, in Lancashire, two years of age, suffered from hernia, and was given over by the medical men. In August, 1883, his mother brought him to the Well, and dipped him in the water. He was cured immediately and completely, and Mr. Howard, a surgeon who had attended him for six months, and saw him afterwards when he was perfectly well, pronounced the cure an evident miracle.

John Tye, a pauper, paralyzed, but able to walk a little with the aid of a stick, was brought to the Well on June 8, 1886. He arrived at nine o'clock in the morning, an hour when only women were accustomed to bathe, and was consequently unable to do so, but was permitted at his own request to dip one foot in the water. He leaped up immediately afterwards, declared himself completely cured, walked and ran, and went away in great joy, thanking God and St. Winefride, and leaving his stick behind him at the Well. He came from Liverpool, but belonged to Wexford, in Ireland. These last two cases are certified by the Father who is now in charge of the mission. He adds accounts of three more cures of recent date. William Ashead, of Altrincham, near Manchester, sixty-two years of age, who had suffered for nearly thirty years from pains and ulcers in his leg, and had spent three months in the infirmary at Manchester, paid three visits to Holywell in 1883, 1884, and 1885, abandoning meanwhile all other attempted remedies. He received some benefit at the first two visits, and at the third was completely cured. He returned in 1886 to give thanks for his recovery. In 1885, he took some of the water away with him, and administered it to an infant two years old, named Alice Bagnell, who was suffering from convulsions. The child recovered at once, and had no return of the malady. Lastly, Catherine Condrick, reduced by spitting blood to such weakness that she was unable to put her arms back and fasten her dress behind her neck, bathed in the Well on June 29, 1886, though she acknowledged she thought a cold bath hardly the best remedy for her complaint. The complaint, nevertheless, ceased from that moment, and her strength soon returned, so that she was able to go about her work as before.

CHAPTER XVII.

Conclusion.

The feast of St. Winefride, 3rd of November, is observed as a lesser double in England, and a double of the first-class in the diocese of Shrewsbury, in which North Wales in included. A Plenary Indulgence is granted by the Holy See to all the faithful who on that day, having confessed and received Holy Communion, visit any church or public oratory and pray for the increase of the true faith in the diocese of Shrewsbury. A Plenary Indulgence may also be gained, any day, by visiting the oratory of St. Winefride, at Holywell, for the same purpose ; and an Indulgence of a hundred days to those who devoutly pray with the same intention before the image of the Saint in the oratory.

English protestants, as a rule, readily and gratefully accept, without cavil, such evidence as is laid before them regarding the continued miraculous powers of St. Winefride's Well in modern times. There are exceptions to this rule, but they are few. Bishop Milner's pamphlet regarding the cure of Winefride White, above noticed, provoked a rejoinder from the Rev. Peter Roberts, A.M., Rector of Llanarmon Dyffryn Ceiriog, and Vicar of Madeley, under the title of *Animadversions on a Pamphlet entitled Authentic Documents*, etc. But the argument of this writer is, in fact, a confirmation of the truth of the history, for he

frankly admits the accuracy of Dr. Milner's state-
ments, on the bishop's authority, but ascribes the
cure of the patient to some occult but natural medicinal property in the water of the Well; a supposition
which, when all the circumstances are considered,
appears nothing less than absurd. Many protestant
writers have recorded the legend of St. Winefride,
such as Bishop Fleetwood, Rees (*Cambro-British
Saints*), Bale, and others; and, as has been seen,
protestants have never been backward in availing
themselves of this means of cure, when brought under
their notice, and when other means have failed.
Thus it points to the truth of a fact which has been
stated and proved on other evidence, that the people
of Great Britain have never, in a proper sense of the
word and of their own accord, abandoned the faith
of their forefathers, nor have ever wholly lost it. The
action of the governments of England and Scotland,
three hundred and fifty years ago, extirpated and
crushed out the Catholic religion, and suppressed it
by force. The people, speaking generally, had no
complicity in this proceeding, did not approve it; so
far as they could, they protested against it. And such
remains of Christian belief as exist among them are
derived from the traditions of other and better days.
Now that just and equitable laws give full freedom
to religious teaching, without fear or favour, it is
surely allowable to hope and pray with confidence
that a thoughtful, honest nation, such as the Welsh
people must be admitted to be, will return one day to
the faith which gave their land so many saints in
ages that are past; saints whose names are necessarily
on their lips every time they speak of a native of
their country, or a town or village in Wales.